Falling Too Soon

Seasons of Love Book One

MICHELE ELIZABETH

Cover Design by Georgia at Pixel and Quill Studio

Line & Copy Edits by Cassie Weaver at Weaver Way Author Services

Formatting by Michele Elizabeth

For all of my fellow basic bitches who love a good PSL and a low hanging pair of gray sweatpants.

PLAYLIST

Need the perfect soundtrack for sweater
weather and stolen kisses?
Check out the <u>Falling Too Soon Playlist</u> on
Spotify:

1

DAPHNE

"Stop!" I screamed. "Just stop. I can't take this anymore." Marcus looked at me as if I had physically wounded him, which was comical because I was all of five-foot nothing and he was a hulk of a man. He was also usually so put together, but in that moment, he appeared to be coming apart at the seams. In all the years we'd been together, I never raised my voice. Never talked back. I had always let him steamroll over me and tried to appease him when his mood was sour.

Not this time.

Not anymore.

Marcus and I had been together for the last four years. Things were tumultuous at best, but I thought I loved him and that he loved me. Shouldn't that have been enough? Our story started like some cliché hospital fairytale—nurse meets doctor, doctor sweeps nurse off her feet. Too bad in our so-called fairytale, the hero turned out to be the villain, and the heroine had to save herself. The thing about Marcus was—he's a master manipulator, charismatic and personable, always the life of the party. Everyone loved him, including my parents, unfortunately. The only person in my life who was anti-Marcus was my bestie, Lexi. She'd been front and center throughout our entire relationship and was constantly telling me I could do better and I should dump his dumb ass.

But here's the problem with dating a narcissist—you're the one who thinks you're wrong all the time. You're overreacting. You're reading too much into it. You're misunderstanding the situation. He made me believe, throughout our entire relationship that I was the problem. And. I. Believed. Him.

What a fucker.

Any who, after a few months of therapy, I finally accepted that I wasn't the problem and decided I had had enough of his manipulation. I was calling it quits and getting the fuck out.

"You really think you can do better than me? Do you think anyone will love you like I do?" Marcus sneered at me. "Who's gonna put up with your ridiculous work hours? Who would deal with your constant nagging?"

I rolled my eyes behind closed eyelids. "Marcus, I'm not happy and I haven't been for a while now. You don't seem to be happy with me anymore, either, like ever. We're always arguing. I just think it's best if we go our separate ways."

"That's because you love to stir the pot, Daphne." My

name sounded like a curse on his lips. "You're always trying to start a fight with me about something. Nothing I do is ever good enough for you!" This was getting us nowhere. I needed to end it once and for all.

"Listen, Marcus, I'm leaving. I don't want to continue this back and forth. I need some space, so I'm going to Lexi's for a while. I'll make arrangements with you to move the rest of my stuff out in a few days when I have a day off." I grabbed my duffle, packed with my essentials, from the side of the couch. Marcus eyed the bag.

"You planned this? You knew you were leaving? This is such a shit move, Daph. I hope you know that this is all your fault. You're the one blowing up our whole fucking life. I was going to propose, you know," he spat.

Oh, fuck this guy.

He was grasping at straws. "Did you seriously think that would make me stay? I said I'm done, and I meant it." My knuckles were white as I gripped the bag tighter and moved toward the door. Marcus moved to block my way, but I lifted my phone out of my pocket to show him I had already been on a call with Lexi.

"Are you fucking for real right now?" He was pissed, his nice guy facade crumbling. "What, did you think I would hurt you or something? You're ridiculous. Just get out of my sight."

I walked out the door, and as he slammed it behind me, I heard Lexi through the speaker on my phone. "You okay, sugar plum?"

"No, but I will be." I was shaking. I couldn't believe I

had actually done it. "I'm on my way over. Thanks again for being on the phone while I did that. I didn't know how he'd react."

"It's no problem, girl. Just drive safe and I'll see you soon," Lexi said as I made my way to my car.

When I arrived at Lexi's apartment, she greeted me at the door with a big glass of wine and an even bigger hug. Gah, I needed both things so freaking bad. It was like I had finally released a breath I'd been holding in for years. Marcus wasn't bad in the beginning. We actually had a lot of fun and had great chemistry, but as time went on, he got more controlling and more confrontational. I felt like I was always walking on eggshells, trying to appease him and smooth things over. I had become a person I didn't even recognize. I was so thankful for Lexi. She was the one who kept me grounded in reality and kept reminding me I wasn't crazy for feeling the way I did. She's actually the one who encouraged me to seek out my therapist too. She's the real MVP.

"Okay, so what's next?" Lexi asked as we got cozy on her couch, a.k.a. my home for the foreseeable future.

"I don't know. Honestly, I've been planning to leave him for a while, but that's where I get stuck. Seeing him at work is going to be hard, I'm sure. I was thinking maybe I should take some time off and get away for a little while to clear my head and make a plan."

Lexi and I were both nurses in a trauma ICU. While I loved being a nurse and the work we did there, it definitely took a toll on me. The ICU could be stressful even on a slow day. There was always something happening—whether it was responding to a code, getting a new admission, patients going to surgery, or family members asking a million questions. I worked twelve-hour shifts, picked up call occasionally, and hadn't been on a real vacation in years, and since Marcus was a workaholic, he and I never went anywhere either. I was definitely due for a break and thought a trip would be the perfect thing to help me get my head straight again.

"That's a great idea! Girls' trip!" Lexi never needed an excuse to take time off work, but I knew a girls' trip with her would involve lots of alcohol and hunting for our next future exes. I had zero interest in looking for men or hooking up. I was looking for the opposite: a week alone to reset, work on myself, and plan what was next for me.

"Actually, I think I need a quiet solo trip to do some soul-searching," I said with a reluctant smile.

Lexi pouted. "Fine, but promise me you'll at least *try* to have fun. And by fun, I mean find yourself a hottie to drown your sorrows in."

I rolled my eyes. "Yeah, that's not happening."

"You're absolutely no fun," Lexi rolled her eyes right back at me.

"Whatever, now help me find a place to stay. I never take vacations, and I have a decent amount of time and money saved up. Let's find a place that looks like it belongs in a magazine." I grabbed my laptop out of my bag and pulled up a vacation rental site to search for that charming town I had seen online. Some girl I followed on social media had posted recently about this cute lake town, a few hours' drive from the city and it looked like something out of a dream—the perfect place for a reset.

We spent the rest of the night drinking, laughing, and searching for the perfect vacation rental for me to escape to.

2

NATHAN

"**B**ut baaaaaaabe," Courtney whined. "It was a one-time thing. It meant nothing!"

I rolled my eyes. We were supposed to be getting married next week and Courtney cheated on me. She fucking cheated on me, and I just felt numb. Shouldn't I be more upset? Why wasn't I more upset? I thought I loved this girl, but I was nowhere near as devastated as I should've been. Maybe I was in shock? Whatever the reason, I was sitting at our kitchen island in our beautiful downtown apartment with my head in my hands, feeling… *was that relief?*

"Courtney, I can't marry someone who would cheat on me. This is a deal breaker for me. I want to be with someone who loves me so much that the thought of being with someone else would make them physically ill. Clearly, that's not the case for you. The wedding is off." We'd been going round and round about this for far too long. There was no way I was continuing a relationship with her after finding out she cheated on me.

I met Courtney, a relatively well-known social media influencer and blogger, at an event a couple of years ago when I was promoting my latest book release. We were immediately attracted to one another, and things got hot and heavy fairly quickly. After only a few months, we moved in together and, after a year of dating, got engaged.

Looking back, I wondered if her attraction was actually to me or my newfound popularity as a bestselling romance author. It seemed real enough at the time, and until recently, I didn't have any major reservations about our relationship. Then, when photos came out of her getting up close and personal with some B-list celebrity at an event last month, we had a huge fight. She swore nothing actually happened and that the pictures were photoshopped.

Yeah right.

Well, I tried to let it go because we were getting married soon and I didn't know for sure if it went further than the pictures showed. It was still bothering me, so I brought it up again this afternoon. That's when Courtney finally came clean. She had slept with the guy from the photo and she thought if she told me the truth, we could move on and I would just get past her indiscretion.

"I don't understand how you could throw away our whole relationship and cancel our wedding for a one-time thing. I thought you'd be able to get past it and we could move on even stronger than before." This girl was delusional if she thought that. "Look, Nate." God, I hated it when she called me that. "We're basically famous. Famous people have affairs. I don't see why you're making such a big deal out of this," she stated so matter-of-factly while tossing her bleach-blonde hair over her shoulder.

What did I ever see in her?

Okay, enough was enough. "Courtney, I don't care if you have seven billion followers. I expect the woman I'm going to spend the rest of my life with to be faithful to me and I to her. I'm done. I'll stay at a hotel for a while, but I'm gonna need you to find somewhere to go."

"You can't be serious! You're kicking *me* out?" She was losing her cool, and I knew what was coming. "Fuck that, Nate! This is my apartment as much as it is yours," she practically screamed. Yeah, forget the fact that my name is on the lease and that I was here before I met her.

"You have one week, Courtney. I think that's pretty generous, considering. I'm going to take some time away, and when I get back, I expect you and your things to be gone." I turned toward our bedroom to pack. Courtney was now sobbing and grabbing at my shirt to stop me. I shrugged out of her grasp and made my way to the bedroom. After packing for a week's stay in a hotel and for what would have been our honeymoon, I walked back out to the kitchen. She didn't even look at me as I grabbed my keys off the island and made my way to the door.

I drove to a hotel not far from our apartment and checked in. When I made it to my room, I flopped onto the bed and opened the group text thread I had with my brothers, Brandon and Dylan.

ME

Looks like you guys were right.

DYLAN

Say that again. I love the way that sounds coming from you.

BRANDON

Ditto.

My brothers were my best friends. We talked all the time, saw each other whenever we could, and gave each other shit like it was our job. Out of the three of us, I was the oldest at thirty-four, then it was Brandon at twenty-nine and Dylan at twenty-seven. We grew up just outside the city in a modest house with two loving parents. Mom stayed home and took care of us when we were small, and as we got older, she helped Dad in our family's tattoo shop. Our parents were madly in love right until cancer took Mom from us six years ago. Their relationship was actually the inspiration for one of my first romance novels. They'd had a love that I had always hoped to find for myself one day.

ME

Listen, assholes, there's no need to rub it in, but Courtney admitted she cheated with that guy. It's over. I ended it and got a room at The Marquis for the week.

DYLAN

Wait a fucking minute... YOU left? Why didn't you make her leave?

God, I knew they'd be pissed that I let her stay in the

apartment. Truth be told, I didn't want to be there, and I was desperate for a change of scenery. We had our honeymoon already booked for next week in a cabin by a lake in a town not too far from the city. Courtney was always talking about going there to vlog about the town in the fall, so I booked it for our honeymoon as a surprise. I figured I might as well still go and hopefully find some inspiration for my next novel.

ME

Because I needed to get out of there. I gave her a week to pack up and find somewhere else to go.

Radio silence. They were probably sitting at the shop together, talking shit instead of texting me back. Dicks.

ME

I'm gonna get out of town for a week and get my head straight. Maybe I'll start my next book. I had planned to take some time off from writing for the wedding and honeymoon, but it looks like I've got time now, soooo…

BRANDON

Where ya goin'?

DYLAN

I hope somewhere where the girls are scantily clad and DTF.

BRANDON

Jesus, Dylan, that is the last thing he
needs. He needs to get his head right, not
get caught up in another woman.

DYLAN

I didn't say get in a relationship—just get
under another hot body to get over this
last one.

ME

God, you are so predictable, Dylan, and
no, I'm not looking to hook up. I'm going
to that lake town Courtney had been
wanting to check out. I booked a week
there on the lake as a surprise for her for
our honeymoon.

DYLAN

You think that will help you get over her?
In the place you were planning on
spending the week balls deep in her?

ME

Thanks for that visual, but no, I don't think
it will be an issue. The place looks so
tranquil; it's the perfect place for
inspiration to strike for my next book.

BRANDON

Well, big bro, I sure hope so! Miss you,
and I'm sorry you're going through this.
Let's get together before you go. Gotta
run; my next appointment is here.
Love ya!

DYLAN

Yeah, what he said. Love ya. See ya soon.

ME

Love you guys too. Talk soon.

THE NEXT DAY, I woke up in a mood. I was definitely not in shock anymore. I was pissed. I felt betrayed. I couldn't understand how anyone could cheat on someone they were supposedly in love with and going to marry. So, I did what anyone in my situation would do. I ordered room service and moped around the hotel room most of the morning. Not exactly how I thought this week was going to go, but I had little to do since I had taken some time off to spend with my girl getting the last-minute wedding details squared away. Now, what was I going to do for a week? Ugh.

I pulled out my laptop and found the booking email for the vacation rental I had reserved for our honeymoon. Maybe I could go early? I knew I didn't want to spend the next week cooped up in this hotel room, so I emailed the property manager to see if it was available. To my surprise, I received a response a few minutes later saying that the house would be available in a few days. Well, that was easy.

Next stop—the quaint town of Lakeside and hopefully some new inspiration.

3

———————

DAPHNE

"Earth to Daphne," Lexi said, pulling me out of my thoughts. I blinked and gave her a soft smile. We were sitting in the break room at work and I was supposed to be guzzling down a snack, but instead, I had been staring off into space. I'd love to say I was just zoned out, but the truth was, I was freaking out. I couldn't believe I actually did it. I left Marcus.

"Babes, you need to eat. We're slammed. You don't have time to spiral right now." Lexi pushed a bag of chips into my hand. She was right, of course. We were busy as shit today and I needed to fuel up.

"You're right. I'm good," I said as I shoved a few chips in my mouth. "I just can't believe I did it."

"Did what?" Amanda asked as she plopped down in the chair next to me and stole a chip from my bag. Amanda was one of the other nurses in the unit and around the same age as Lexi and me.

"She left Marcus last night," Lexi responded with a little too much excitement.

"No fucking way." Amanda's eyes were wide as she snatched another chip. "Way to go. I'm proud of you. How'd he take it? Have you seen him today?"

"No, I haven't seen him, and I don't plan to. I'm actually trying to take a few days off and get out of town. I hope Jess lets me take some time off."

"I can help cover for you," Amanda replied. "I could use the extra shifts. I'm saving for a vacation myself."

"Thanks, girl. I'll let her know when I ask her later." I pushed back from the table and stood. "I gotta get back out there."

My assignment for the day was a single, ventilated patient with a traumatic brain injury and a few fractures from a motorcycle accident who had been in the ICU for a few days now. Since our lovely state didn't have a helmet law, he was in pretty bad shape when he came in. Thankfully, he'd already come through the worst of it and we were just starting to wean him off his sedation.

"I'm back," I said to Jamie, one of the resource nurses, as I approached the room.

"Not much to report. I changed your insulin drip and emptied the Foley. Everything is documented," Jamie replied. "I'll check back on ya later." She gave me a wave and moved on to the next room.

My patient's wife looked up and gave me a small smile from where she sat at her husband's bedside. That's where she'd been almost every minute of visiting hours since he was admitted, holding his hand, telling him that she was there, letting him know everything would be okay. I think that was the hardest part of my job. It wasn't the blood or dealing with death—it was the families. Seeing my patients' families sobbing and struggling with their new normal was hard for me. I always imagined myself in their position… what was it like loving someone so much that you wished you could trade places with them? I shook that thought from my mind—I had work to do.

I walked into the room, stopped next to my patient's wife and placed a hand on her shoulder. "How are you holding up?"

"I've been better." She gave me another weak smile that didn't quite reach her eyes. "I don't know what I'd do without him. He's my whole world." A tear trailed down her cheek.

I reached for the box of tissues that were on the bedside table and offered her one. "I can only imagine what you're going through."

Taking care of the families was just as much a part of my job as taking care of the patients. There was a fine line when it came to offering reassurances, though. I couldn't say things like "everything will be okay" or "he'll pull through" because the truth of the matter was, I didn't know if everything would be all right or if he would, in fact, pull through.

"I just keep thinking, what if he doesn't wake up? What if he's not the person I married when he does?" Another tear broke free.

I rubbed her back. "Just try to focus on the positives right now. His scans have improved and we're weaning his sedation. That's all good news."

"You're right. I'll try." She looked up at me with more unshed tears still in her eyes. "I think I'm going to go grab some coffee. I'll be back in a little while."

"Take your time. I'll be here with him." I gave her a reassuring squeeze as she stood.

"I know you will be, and I appreciate you so much." She leaned down to kiss her husband and whispered, "I love you. I'll be right back."

She left and tears built behind my eyes, but I held them back and got back to work. I always had big feelings when dealing with family members, especially with my really sick patients. But I had to push those feelings aside and focus on the clinical side of my job. I saved my emotional breakdowns for my biweekly shower cries like a normal person. I needed to be strong at work and have a clear head.

THE NEXT COUPLE of days were a blur. We were so busy at work that I barely had time to eat, let alone think about my life and how much of a disaster it was. Caring for critically ill patients and their families could be my sole focus while at work. My patient did wake up and, thankfully, was neurologically the same man he had been before his accident. Physically, he still had a long road ahead of him, but he was stable and would hopefully be out of the ICU soon.

While I wouldn't wish having to be in the ICU on anyone, I was thankful for the distraction from my life and that I hadn't had any run-ins with Marcus. He was a urologist in the same hospital, but we rarely crossed paths throughout the day unless we did so intentionally for lunch or a quickie in an on-call room—not my finest moments, but hey, a girl has needs.

After those few hectic days at work, I was even more excited about my trip. I was more than ready for a break. Fortunately, Lexi and I had found the perfect cabin right on the lake. It was positively Instagram-worthy but also cost more than I would ordinarily spend. Sure, I kind of blew my load on it, but YOLO, right? I was even able to get time off from work without having to pitch a fit, which was unexpected but also very much appreciated. Word had gotten around about Marcus and me, and I think my manager felt bad for me. Whatever. I'd take it.

4

DAPHNE

The day before I was set to leave for my trip, I stopped by Marcus's place while I knew he'd be at work and cleared out the rest of my things. I didn't have much there since almost everything was already there when I moved in. All I had to pack was the rest of my clothes and a few things I had in the building storage area downstairs. I dropped everything off in a storage locker I had rented and then headed out on my week-long vacation to rest and regroup.

The drive to Lakeside was breathtaking. It was early October, and the leaves had just started to change. Red, orange, and yellow painted the landscape as I wound through hills and valleys on my way to my destination. Fall was my absolute favorite time of year. I loved everything about it—the cooler temperatures, the changing leaves, the availability of pumpkin spice everything. Lakeside was the perfect place to visit this time of year, boasting a quaint main street lined with trees, photo-worthy shops, and a charming little bookstore that I couldn't wait to check out.

I stopped by a market on the outskirts of town to grab the essentials—coffee, my favorite pumpkin spice creamer, wine, and a few snacks. I'd deal with getting real food tomorrow. At that moment, I just wanted to get to the cabin, start a fire in that cozy fireplace I had been eye-balling in the online photos, open a bottle of wine, and curl up with my book.

As I pulled onto the gravel drive that led to the cabin, I was taken aback by how gorgeous it was in real life. The A-frame cabin sat perched on the edge of the lake with a wall of windows looking out over it. The sun was setting behind the cabin—solar torches lined the driveway, and several exterior lights cast a warm glow. It was like looking at a postcard. At that moment, I definitely did not regret spending the extra money on this lakefront beauty. As I parked in front of the cabin, I noticed smoke coming from the chimney. Did the property manager come and start the fire for me? Wow, nice touch! I guess it pays to splurge.

I grabbed the grocery bag and bottle of wine and headed toward the door. The rest of my stuff would have to wait—wine was the priority, after all. As I keyed in the door code provided in my confirmation email, I thought I heard a sound coming from inside. Brushing it off, I swung open the door and walked in. There were a few lights on, and I could smell the fire burning in the fireplace. I walked down a short hallway into the main living area and was startled by a crashing sound. Dazed, I looked down, only to realize it was my wine that had shattered and made a huge mess on the floor where my jaw was now resting.

I raised my eyes to see a god of a man wearing nothing but a pair of low-hanging gray sweatpants and a grin. *Fuck me. Why's it gotta be gray sweatpants?* It was as if I'd walked into my very own meet-cute. Maybe I should lay off the romance novels.

The Adonis that stood before me did, in fact, look like he belonged on the cover of one of my books. His hair was dark and tousled, like he'd been running his hands through it. He had a slight amount of stubble on his face that made me want to feel it against my thighs. *Oh my God, Daphne, get it together.* His chest and abs were fully on display, with a few tattoos on his chest and arm that seemed to fit him perfectly. This man was hot with a capital T. He definitely spent time in the gym and it showed. As my gaze raked up his chiseled six-foot-who-knows-how-tall body and my eyes zeroed in on his, I think I stopped breathing. His eyes were lighter than I would have expected, despite the rest of his dark features, and he was wearing glasses that made him look infinitely hotter, as if that were even possible.

"Can I help you?" the stranger asked amusedly as I tried to pick my jaw up off the floor.

"Oh, shit!" I shrieked. "Shit, shit, shit," I continued while I scrambled to pick up the grocery items that were now all over the ground. The handsome stranger approached and crouched down to help me. Our hands touched, and I swear I felt that touch all the way in my toes. When I looked up at him again, I froze and my mouth returned to its afore-mentioned position of agape.

"Hey, are you okay?" He was looking at me as if I were a lunatic. Maybe I was. Was I in the wrong place?

"Shit, sorry, yeah. Um, I may have the wrong place. God, I'm so sorry. Let me check." I dropped the groceries I was trying to clean up and pulled out my phone. *Wait, I used the code to get in. This has to be the right place,* I thought. I pulled up the confirmation email and checked the address and door code. *Yep, I was in the right place.* "Um, I have this confirmation email," I said as I turned my phone to face him. He'd put my groceries back into the bag, minus the broken wine that was now a lost cause.

"Hmm, yeah, that's this place, but I just checked in yesterday." He stood, holding out my bag to me. "Looks like they double-booked. Wait right there. I'm gonna grab something to clean this up."

Could I be more of a disaster? I was standing here eye-fucking this guy, not doing a damn thing to help clean up the mess I made. "No, please let me help; it's my mess." I started to follow him and then stopped myself. This was a stranger. I was in a fairly secluded cabin in the woods with a stranger. I didn't feel unsafe, but maybe I should have. Alarm bells should've been ringing so loud in my head, yet there I was, trying to follow him deeper into the cabin.

Use your brain, Daphne.

He was on his way back with a broom, cleaning spray,

and paper towels when he said, "No, really, it's okay. Stay there. There's glass all over and I don't want you to hurt yourself." *What a gentleman. Shut up, Daphne, he could be a serial killer.*

I stood there like a lump on a log while hottie McSweatpants cleaned up my mess. When he finished and smiled up at me from his position on the floor, I was still staring at him like an idiot. *Sweet baby Cheesus, help me.*

"Well, come on in and let's figure this out," he said, oh so nonchalantly. *Couldn't he tell I was losing my shit? How was he so calm?* In a daze, I followed him—*still no alarm bells*—into the open living area and to the kitchen island, where I placed my grocery bag, wishing now more than ever that my wine had been spared.

"Can I get you something to drink?" I blinked at him. God, he must have thought I was daft. I couldn't even form sentences. What was wrong with me? I was an educated, articulate woman, for Christ's sake. Shaking myself out of my ab-induced coma, I nodded.

"I have bourbon? Or I think I saw a bottle of wine somewhere in here. Maybe some water?" He started to turn to face the cabinets.

"Bourbon is great." *What the fuck Daphne, since when do you drink bourbon? Since now, that's when.*

The still half-naked stranger—*why was he still shirtless?*—turned and grabbed a glass from the cabinet, added a couple of cubes of ice from the freezer, and poured in some brown liquid that I had to assume was bourbon. He slid it across the island to me, and I grasped onto it like it was a lifeline and took a hefty swig. *Shit, that burns.* I started coughing a little but mostly kept my shit together.

"I'm Nathan." His voice was deep and sexy as hell, and yep, I was totally fucking fucked.

5

NATHAN

Fucking stunning. That's the first thing that came to mind when I saw her. Well, maybe that was the second thing I thought. The first was more likely. *What the fuck?* After all, there was a huge mess in the entry hall and a gorgeous woman along with it.

After her initial freak out and me cleaning up the mess while she remained mostly dazed, I offered her a drink and topped mine off. She stared into her glass of bourbon as if it held all the answers to life's mysteries and clung to it as if it would disappear at any moment. "Are you okay?" I asked for the second time since she had invaded my space.

"Yeah, sorry. I was a little caught off guard when I saw you standing there. I wasn't expecting anyone to be here. Is your car outside? Did I totally miss it?" She was now looking straight into my eyes. Her amber orbs pierced my soul. She was petite but curvy, with long brown hair that had little hints of caramel. She was wearing a cropped sweatshirt and black leggings that showcased her hourglass figure. Her skin was pale and looked so damn soft. I wanted to curl up next to her in a bed and never leave.

Who said that? You do not want to get in bed with this girl. You were just engaged like five minutes ago.

"Yeah, it's no problem. I was just as shocked to see you here too. As for the car, it's off on the side of the cabin, so I'm not surprised you missed it." I wanted to know more about her. "So what's your name? As I said, I'm Nathan."

"Oh shit, sorry, I'm Daphne."

Daphne.

"Yeah, so I don't know what to do here. I'm assuming you have a confirmation email too or something?" She got right down to business, pulling me out of my daydream of snuggling up next to her by the fire. *What?*

"I do. And I checked in yesterday, like I said." I went to grab my phone from where I had left it by the fire in the now too-hot living room. *Was it getting hotter in here?* It most definitely felt hotter. I pulled up my confirmation email to show her. Yep, we were double-booked. I'm sure my last-minute change to my reservation was the culprit, but I wasn't about to tell her that.

"Well, you were here first," she started, "so I guess let me see what I can find online for the night." She started searching on her phone for accommodations. Under her breath and barely audible, she sighed, "Of fucking course, this is just my fucking luck." She scrolled on her phone for a beat and then, as if remembering something, dropped the phone to her side and huffed.

"What is it?" I asked. She hadn't been scrolling long enough to not find something.

"They charged me for this place already, and it wasn't cheap. I don't know if I can get something else until they refund my payment." Her eyes were glassy. God, I hope she didn't cry. I grew up with brothers and a mother who was tough as nails. I was not equipped to handle a crying stranger in my cabin, even a beautiful one. She continued, "It's fine, I'll figure something out," and started to turn and head for the door. "Thanks for the dr—"

I didn't think I just moved. My hand was on her arm before I could stop myself. She stopped and stared at me like I was insane. Maybe I was. All I knew was that, at that moment, I didn't want her to leave. I had no business touching her or doing what I did next, yet there I was.

"Stay."

6

DAPHNE

"Excuse me?" His strong hand gripped my arm, his touch firm but gentle. When my eyes met his, I knew I was a fucking goner. He was looking at me like I was a goddamn snack and he was starving. His breathing was heavier. My brain must have glitched because all I could think was, "God, I hope he kisses me." *Where the hell did that come from?* Oh yeah, I know, that was my treacherous pussy chiming in. The one who desperately needed attention since Marcus had not been the most generous of lovers, and, if I was being honest, I had been avoiding having sex with him for at least the last month while I built up the courage to leave.

Nathan licked his lips and dragged his gaze from my eyes to my mouth, down my body and back up. My breath hitched, and I bit down on my lower lip. I guess that was his invitation because, the next thing I knew, his mouth was on mine, and he was kissing me, and I was letting it happen.

He wasn't timid or soft. His kiss was hard and demanding, and when his tongue brushed against my lips, I parted them for him. Well, shit, this guy could kiss. One of his hands traveled up into my hair at the back of my head, where he pulled slightly to expose my neck. His mouth was hot and wet as he dragged it from mine down my neck. My hands were against his chest. Was I trying to pull him closer or push him away? I wasn't sure. A moan escaped me as he pulled back and his eyes met mine again. We stared at each other for a moment before he released my hair and took a reluctant step back.

"Shit, I'm sorry," he said as he dragged a hand through his hair. "I don't know what came over me." I tried to compose myself, but that seemed like an impossible task.

"That was…intense. And unexpected," I said as I brought my fingers up to touch my lips, my breathing labored. I shook my head. "Do you make a habit of sticking your tongue into every stranger who walks into your house uninvited?"

Nathan smirked and let out a little chuckle. God, if that wasn't the hottest thing I'd ever heard. "No, but it's not every day that the sexiest woman I've ever seen breaks in and tosses a bottle of wine at me."

I snorted, "Listen, I didn't *toss* anything. I was just shocked to see someone here. And I don't know if you've looked in a mirror yet today, but holy hell. I definitely wasn't expecting all of this." I held out my hands, gesturing to his body. My eyes trailed down his form, admiring the deep V that disappeared into his low-slung sweatpants and down to his… Oh. My. God. He was hard, and the outline of his very large erection was difficult to miss. I could have seen that monster from space.

He laughed and I swear it shot straight to my clit. The effect that this man was having on me was unreal.

"Okay, okay. Look, I'm sorry I attacked you, but you're gorgeous, and I think my brain short-circuited there for a minute. I'm all right now. Why don't you come back and sit down? We'll figure something out."

"Then you may want to go find a shirt before my brain short-circuits again too." Lies. My brain was already totally fucked. All I wanted to do was peel those damn gray sweatpants off and lick this man from head to fucking toe.

Smiling, he turned his back to me and said, "Okay, I'll go make myself less of a temptation so we can figure out our housing situation." He disappeared down another hallway, and I let out a breath. I headed back to the kitchen and finished the rest of my bourbon. I had a feeling I was gonna need it.

7

NATHAN

Fuck me. Where did this woman come from, and what did she do to my freaking brain? It was as if I was no longer in control of my body, and all I could think about was getting her naked and into my bed pronto, but that should've been the furthest thing from my mind. I just got out of a serious relationship. I was engaged, for crying out loud. I was supposed to have been getting married in a few short days.

I pulled on an old, beat-up T-shirt and tried to calm my raging hard-on. Holy shit, Daphne was so damn sexy, and that kiss. Fuck me, that kiss was hot, and clearly, my dick thought so too. There was no way that Daphne hadn't noticed my poorly timed erection, but there was nothing to do about that now. When I was sure it wasn't so noticeable, I headed back to the kitchen, where Daphne had finished her bourbon. That sounded like a great idea. I needed more booze too.

As I stepped up to the kitchen island, she turned to me and smiled a smile that I swear lit up the whole damn room.

Holding her hand out to me, she said, "Hi, I'm Daphne. It's nice to meet you." I chuckled and shook my head.

This woman.

I grasped her small, warm hand in mine, brought her knuckles up, and grazed them with my lips. "The pleasure is all mine," I said as I glanced up into eyes I could get lost in. "I'm Nathan."

"Seriously, my guy? Could you not?" She laughed. "It's like you can't help but be sexy. Are you sure you're not a character from one of my books?"

I choked a bit on my drink. "Well, I guess that depends on what kind of books you're reading. I *am* a romance author."

"Of course you are," she said, rolling her eyes. "Lucky me, ending up all alone in a cabin with a sexy stranger who just so happens to know exactly what to do and say to make a woman swoon."

"You're making me sound like a predator, which I'm not, by the way," I snickered. "Want another?" I gestured toward her now-empty glass.

She rolled her eyes again but held her glass out to me. "Why not? It's not like this can get any weirder." She chuckled as she pulled out her phone and I refilled her glass. "I gotta text my friend and let her know I'm okay for now. Just know I'm letting her know that if she doesn't receive proof of life within the next hour, to alert the local authorities." She pointed a finger in my direction. "You've been warned, mister. No murdering me and burying me in these woods.

She's funny. I like her. *Do you hear yourself, man? Get your shit together. This is no time to be liking anyone.* She shot off a quick text and then put her phone face down on the counter. "So what are you doing up here in this cabin all alone, anyway? Are you meeting someone?" I was so curious about her.

"The smart thing to do would be to lie and tell you that my beefy boyfriend is joining me soon, but for reasons I don't quite understand, I don't want to lie to you, so the truth is…" She sucked in and let out a deep breath. "I just broke things off with my boyfriend, who was a complete piece of shit. I booked this vacation rental to escape my life for a while and figure out what's next for me. What about you? Why are *you* up here all alone? I'm still not convinced you're not a serial killer or something." She raised an eyebrow and took another swig of her drink.

"Actually, my story is pretty similar to yours, believe it or not." She waited as I took a sip and then continued, "This was supposed to be my honeymoon, but my fiancé cheated on me and I broke things off. Came up here to clear my head, maybe start my next book."

"Shit, I'm so sorry. That's awful. And you're not feeling weird about staying here alone when you were supposed to be here with her?" She looked concerned, her brows furrowed.

"It is what it is, I guess. It's a beautiful place, and I'm hoping it inspires a new story." I shrugged. "You hungry?"

"It's almost eight," she announced, looking at me like I was crazy for suggesting food at this hour. "Anyway, I think I'd better sort out where I'm staying tonight."

"Stay here." That look that she had given me, the one that told me she thought I was nuts, intensified. Maybe I was nuts, but I knew I wanted more time with her. As crazy as that sounded, it was the only thing that made sense to me at that moment.

"Oh no, you were here first. I couldn't possibly take your rental now. I'm sure I can find something cheap in town for the night."

"Look, there's more than one bedroom, so we can both be comfortable, and I'm sure there are locks on the doors, so I won't be able to come in and kill you while you sleep." I smirked. This girl seemed smart. There's no way she was going to stay, but I had to try. I needed to know her, if only for one night.

"This is crazy, right? Any sane person would have already left. Clearly, you got me on an off day because I'm actually considering this." She shook her head as she held out her glass for another refill. Although refill may have been an exaggeration, seeing how I was only pouring in a shot each time.

"Oh, come on, this'll be fun! We can commiserate together. What could possibly go wrong?" I joked.

A few bourbons later, we were sprawled out on the couch watching some scary movie that Daphne had put on and munching on popcorn. We had already done the small talk thing and had kept things pretty surface-level prior to putting on the movie. I wasn't watching the movie, though. I was watching her. She was exquisite. The warm glow of the fire made the caramel parts of her hair glow and her honey-colored eyes sparkle. Her cheeks were pink. It could have been from the warmth of the fire or the booze. It didn't matter. I wanted to touch them, caress them, feel my lips against them. This was so wrong. Why was I so drawn to this woman?

When she turned to look at me and caught me staring, she smiled. "What?"

I think the bourbon was working because my filter was gone. "You are gorgeous." I think I saw her already pink cheeks blush.

"Thank you." She smiled sweetly and turned back to the movie, trying to avoid my eyes.

Fuck it. I was going in. She seemed into that kiss we shared earlier, and it's all I'd thought about since. That small moan that left her lips as mine brushed over her neck was intoxicating. I felt the need to know what she sounded like when she came, and I wanted to hear my name on her lips as she lost control.

I inched myself a little closer to her on the couch and reached my hand further to close the distance. With my hand almost touching her thigh, she repositioned herself and moved slightly in my direction. Just enough that my hand grazed her thigh.

Oh fuck yeah, it was so on.

8

───────

DAPHNE

I saw, in my periphery, that Nathan had moved closer, and boy, did I want him even closer still. We had been watching a movie, but I wasn't paying it any attention. I was so focused on steadying my breathing and trying to keep my cool, but it wasn't working. I was on fire. Even though Nathan put on a shirt, it did absolutely nothing to dull how attractive he was. If anything, it made him infinitely hotter. The thin, worn T-shirt clung to him like a second skin. I could see every muscle as if he had nothing on at all.

And then there were those damn sweatpants. I tried not to look. I swear on my love of all things pumpkin spice that I tried to keep my eyes to myself. But listen, this man was blessed in the package department, and it was impossible not to notice. He wasn't even hard, but the outline of his softish cock had me drooling.

Nathan was so close he could almost reach out and touch me. I made a show of "adjusting my position" to inch my way toward him, to close the distance until his hand brushed my thigh. That was all it took for my restraint to go right out the door, where I should have gone as soon as I realized I wasn't alone in this house. Yet here I was, letting myself give in to my desire for him. It had been years since I had a one-night stand, and dammit, I deserved this.

My eyes snapped to his, and we stared at each other hungrily. It was like earlier, right before that first kiss. Everything felt as if it moved in slow motion, yet he was on me in an instant.

He grabbed my face between his powerful hands placed his forehead to mine while breathing me in. "Tell me to stop, Daphne." His crumbling restraint was evident in his voice.

"Don't you dare," I breathed as we fell into each other. His hands were everywhere. His tongue attacked my mouth completely unrestrained. I pulled his shirt up and over his head and took my time running my hands over the smooth skin of his chest. Sliding my hands down, I ran a finger over each dip of his abs.

Jesus, did he live in the gym?

His hands felt so good on me. Everywhere he touched sent electric shocks throughout my body. My body hummed, but I wanted more.

His hands moved under my top, sliding up further until his fingers brushed under the bottom edge of my bra. I arched into him while he reached around to unfasten it. With my next breath, he was lifting my top over my head and tossing it and my bra to the ground. Bare before him from the waist up, he took a moment to look at me. "Daphne, you are a fucking goddess," he said breathlessly as he moved back into my space, pushing me against the couch.

He moved his body over mine and captured my mouth with his again. With one arm bracing himself by my head and one hand on my rib cage, he pressed into me. I could feel how hard he was now, grinding into me, driving me crazy with need. He broke our kiss to move his lips to my neck. The hand on my ribs moved over my breast, and his thumb grazed my nipple. I was a writhing, whimpering mess. He continued his trek down my body and stopped to suck a stiff nipple into his mouth while rolling the other between his fingers. I let out a yelp and drove my hips up into him. I wanted more, and I would take everything he wanted to give me.

"More. Nathan, I need more," I mewled, as he continued to toy with me.

"I love it when you say my name. Tell me what you need," he whispered against my chest.

"I need you to touch me."

"Daphne, I'm going to need you to be more specific. What do you need?" Okay, now he was just fucking with me. He knew what I wanted, but he was making me say it. I had never been very vocal in the bedroom before. Even though I was exposed intimately, I felt so self-conscious talking during sex. But fuck it, I'd probably never see this guy again, so why not act the part of a confident sex goddess for once?

"Nathan, I want you to touch my pussy." I could feel

him smile against me. *Fuck yes!* That small thing made me feel so powerful. His hands moved further down, and he pulled down my leggings and thong in one motion. He backed up to pull off my booties and get my bottoms the rest of the way off. I was completely bare to him, and the look on his face was something I wanted to remember for the rest of my life. I truly felt like the goddess I was pretending to be at that moment.

His eyes continued to rake over my body, admiring me like I was a piece of art, while he rubbed his hands over my thighs. My legs fell open slightly, drawing his gaze to my now aching center. "Look at you, so wet for me already," he said as he licked his lips and reached to swipe his thick fingers through my folds. When he brought his fingers to his mouth, I stopped breathing. My eyes were wide as he put his fingers coated in my arousal into his mouth and sucked. *Holy shit.*

"Fucking delicious." Without taking a breath, his head was between my thighs, placing too gentle kisses on my inner thigh, to the left of my pussy, on my—thankfully recently waxed—mound just above where I wanted him. I was convulsing, moving my hips erratically, trying to get him where I needed him when he swiped his thumb through my dripping center and then started to circle my clit with it. He was still peppering kisses on my thighs and had his other hand reaching up to play with my tits. When he increased his pressure and speed on my clit, I came undone. My orgasm came fast and hard. I don't think I'd ever had an orgasm that fast in my entire life. He continued to rub my sensitive bud as I came down, and while I was still reeling through the aftershocks, he swiped his thick, flat tongue through my wetness and over my clit.

"Oh my God," I shouted as I grabbed his head. "You don't have to do that."

"Have to? In what universe would this be a chore? Eating your sweet pussy is a fucking privilege, and I would sooner die than stop before I've had my fill."

The mouth on this man. He continued to eat me as if I was his last meal. He sucked my clit into his mouth and tugged while pushing one of his thick fingers into me. I gasped at the intrusion. I'd gone completely feral, moaning and panting like I was possessed. My hands gripped his dark locks for dear life as I ground my pussy into him.

"That's right, Baby, let go. I want you to come all over me. Soak me." Oh, fuck! He added a second finger. The stretch was almost too much, but also not enough. He pumped them in and out of me faster while licking and sucking on my already sensitive clit. I screamed and called Nathan's name like he could somehow save me from myself.

My next orgasm was something otherworldly, and there was a sensation I'd never felt before. I felt a gush of something wet as I came so hard I saw stars. I had no idea what was happening, but I was flying too high to care. I could feel my clit pulsing and sending shockwaves throughout my body. I was panting and trying to catch my breath as Nathan made one final swipe of his tongue through me and then trailed sweet, lazy kisses back up my body. He only stopped to worship each of my breasts and lick my nipples before reaching my mouth, where he graced me with the most sensual kiss I think I'd ever experienced. The taste of me on him made it that much more. I was lost in him. In that kiss.

"Baby, that was so hot. Who would have thought you were a squirter?" I blink up at him. *A what? No fucking way.* I was mortified and started to cover my face with my hands. "Don't you dare be embarrassed. That was the hottest thing I've ever experienced."

"That's never happened before. I…I didn't even know I could do that," I admitted as he slowly released my hands and started to get off the couch. I felt the loss of his weight against me immediately. When I looked up at him standing above me, I could see he was hard, the outline of his—probably too big for me—cock straining against the confines of those fucking gray sweatpants. My mouth watered at the sight. There was no way that was gonna fit in me, but I was determined to try.

Suddenly, I was being thrown over his shoulder like a rag doll as he marched us to his room. He tossed me down onto the bed, and as he slid his pants down and kicked them away, I think I actually drooled at the sight of him. "See something you like, Daphne? Crawl over here and take it," he growled, pulling me out of my cock-induced coma.

I was feeling bold, more so than I had been before, so I did as he asked. I crawled to the edge of the bed, looking him in the eyes. His eyes were hooded, and his gaze never left mine as I made my way to him. When I reached the edge, I sat back on my heels and ran my hands up his legs, past his rock-hard and intimidating-as-hell cock, and over his tight abs. His breathing was ragged.

Then, as I took his velvety erection in my hand, I marveled at how smooth it was. Wetting my lips slightly, I looked up into Nathan's eyes as I licked his pre-cum from his tip with a flat tongue. The groan that escaped him was almost enough to make me come again, so I reached between my legs with my free hand to touch myself. For that, I was rewarded with, "Fuuuuuck, Baby. Yes. Play with that sweet pussy of yours. Make yourself come for Daddy," from Nathan. *Daddy? Was I into that?* Yep, my whore of a vajayjay let me know we were all in on that shit.

I took him into my throat until I gagged, earning me another deep groan from Nathan. "Baby, if you keep that up, I'm going to come in that pretty mouth of yours. Is that what you want, Daphne? You want me to coat your throat with my cum?" Welp, that did me in. I was coming so hard on my fingers that I barely registered him gripping the back of my head, forcing me further down on his length. I gagged again, but he didn't let up. Tears sprang to my eyes. I must have looked like a raccoon with my mascara running down my face, but I didn't care. I was trying my best to breathe through my nose while he was relentlessly fucking my throat, and I continued to strum my clit. His pace increased and I could tell he was close, so I doubled down on my efforts, taking him higher and higher until he shouted out some words that I couldn't make out as he shot ropes of hot cum into my mouth and down my throat. I swallowed every last drop and then licked his shaft clean. Another first for me.

Who the fuck was I even?

I leaned back on my heels again and wiped under my eyes and across my chin, trying to clean myself up a bit. It was probably pointless, but I tried anyway. Nathan's head was still tilted upward to the ceiling, and he was glistening with a layer of sweat. He looked like a god, and I wished I could worship him daily, but I had to remind myself that this was a one-time thing. Might as well enjoy it while it lasted.

Nathan's eyes shifted to mine as he lowered his head and pushed me back against the bed. Surely he wasn't ready to go again. He had just come, but he was still hard and getting harder by the second. He climbed over me and started kissing me with a renewed hunger. I was so needy and moved my hips against his. His tip slid through my dripping folds and against my clit. His fingers were teasing my nipples as he said in between kissing me, "I need to be inside you, but I don't have any condoms."

Thank fuck, Lexi is a true friend and a total fuck girl because she had thrown a handful in my purse before I left her apartment, hoping I would, in fact, find myself in this exact situation. "I have some," I gasped. "In my purse. Go."

I don't know if I'd ever seen a man move that fast in my entire life and I couldn't help the giggle that escaped me. Nathan was off and running to the kitchen, where my purse was sitting on the island, and back before I could move a muscle. He returned with a sleeve of condoms and a grin. *This fucking guy.*

He stood above me, saying things that no man has ever said to me, words of praise, words of worship, as he sheathed himself with a condom. Then he was hovering over me, supporting his weight with his arms next to my head. He kissed me again while rubbing his length along my swollen clit before oh-so-slowly sliding inside of me. He was big, bigger than I had ever been with, but thankfully, he took his time, allowing me to adjust to his size. He reached down to strum my clit when he finally bottomed out, and I think I had an out-of-body experience.

"You're so tight, Kitten." *Kitten? Did I like that?* My pussy throbbed. *Yep. Sure did.* "Such a good girl taking all of me like this," he groaned against my neck. "Baby, I don't know if I can be gentle."

"Then don't be. I want you to fuck me, Nathan." And with that, the beast was unleashed. Nathan fucked me so hard I thought I'd be split in half. He continued punishing my pussy while whispering filthy things in my ear. He went from licking my neck to kissing me hard. We moved together so well, and after the initial shock of his size, it felt as if we were made to fit together. I could feel myself tightening around him with every thrust. I was so close, and I could tell he was too. His movements were becoming erratic and when I came, I felt him stiffen with his release before collapsing on top of me.

After a few moments, he rolled me over so I was on top of him, rubbed my back, and stroked my hair out of my face. He caught my chin between his fingers to lift it toward him and kissed my nose. "Perfect." That moment felt very intimate, too intimate. I rested my head on his chest, breathing in his scent of bourbon and citrus and sex. I felt so comfortable in his embrace, and I wanted to stay there forever, but nope. Gotta go.

I pushed up off him and he caught my wrist in his hand, "Where do you think you're going?" He tried to pull me back into him.

"Just gotta hit the bathroom. BRB," I said awkwardly and pointed a thumb toward his en suite. I was desperate to get out of there. While one-night stands weren't my thing, I had to remember that was exactly what this was, and cuddling was definitely off the table.

"Okay, but hurry back," Nathan sighed and released me, rolling over onto his side.

I would not be hurrying back. I took my time using the toilet, splashing some water on my face, and trying to fix the mess my mascara made. When some time had passed, I braved cracking the door to the en suite to find Nathan snoring softly.

After making my escape, I stopped in the living room, quickly put my clothes back on, and grabbed my phone. *Shit, how long had we been at it?* I had to text Lexi before she sent the police over here. There was already a text from her and a missed call.

LEXI

Bitch, you'd better have that man balls deep in you and not be dead at the bottom of the lake.

ME

I'm alive, thanks for nothing. I could have been dead and all you care about is if I'm getting some ass?

It was late, and I didn't expect a response, so I got the rest of my stuff from the car and then settled into the other room for the night. I'd worry about where I was going to stay for the rest of the week in the morning.

9

NATHAN

I woke up grinning into my pillow, but as I reached across the bed, I was met by cool, empty sheets. Where was Daphne? Shit, was that a dream? I didn't drink *that* much, did I?

Fuck, I hoped she hadn't left. Last night was incredible, and I was very freaking interested in doing that again and again and again.

Did I need to be rushing into something with someone new? Absolutely not, but I was immediately drawn to her in a way I had never felt before. I didn't know where things would lead, but I knew I was not ready to let her go just yet. I had to learn more about this beautiful creature who had come crashing into my life.

I peeled myself out of bed and, after using the bathroom, walked into the main living area. I could see her car through the front window. Knowing she was still here gave me an instant sense of relief, so my next priority was to make some coffee and text my brothers. I needed help.

ME

Guys, something happened last night and I need advice.

BRANDON

What's up?

ME

I met someone…

BRANDON

You met someone while alone in a cabin in the woods? How? Where? What happened?

DYLAN

Fuck yeah! I told you to go get you some.

ME

Jesus Dylan, calm down, it's not like that. I guess the rental was double-booked, and she just walked in and…idk my brain stopped working. She's beautiful and funny and shit. Things happened, but I need to know more about her. Is this crazy? I've never felt this sort of instant connection before.

The next messages came in at almost the same time.

DYLAN

Yes, this is crazy, but I'm glad you're getting your dick wet—tell me you're getting your dick wet?

BRANDON

Yes, this is crazy! Wtf are you doing, brother? You need to be focusing on you and getting over Courtney, not trying to jump into something with someone new.

How were my brothers so different? Brandon was so levelheaded and honestly, I think he was a hopeless romantic at heart, even though he himself had yet to find love. He really rooted for me and Courtney, especially at the beginning of our relationship. Then there was Dylan, the consummate "player" who swears he'd never settle down. He never liked Courtney. Maybe he was a better judge of character than Brandon and me.

ME

Guys, look, I don't know what's going on with us, but the chemistry between us was off the charts. She just got out of a relationship too, so I don't want to spook her. I want to get to know her to see if there could be something there.

BRANDON

Well, I say go for it. It is batshit crazy, but you never know—this could end up like one of your books. Try not to rush things though, be her friend. I'm sure she could use one of those right now and so could you.

DYLAN

How am I related to you two?

I heard the door to her room open and steps coming

toward the kitchen, where the smell of coffee was now wafting through the space.

ME

Thanks for the advice Brando and thanks for nothing, as usual, Dylan. Love you guys. I gotta go. I think she's up.

I was smiling like an idiot as she rounded the corner and practically jumped out of her skin, clutching her hand to her chest when she saw me. "Good morning." I smirked at her, and damn if she didn't look adorable. Her hair was piled up on top of her head in a messy bun, and she had on an over-sized hoodie with black leggings and a pair of fuzzy slippers. She still looked half asleep and clearly wasn't expecting me to be in the kitchen.

"Shit, you're up early. Morning," she murmured as she gestured to the coffee. "Can I get some of that?"

"With your creamer?" I asked her as I retrieved two cups from the cupboard.

"How did you…" I poured her a steaming cup and turned to grab her creamer from the fridge.

"I saw it when I was picking up your groceries. But pumpkin spice?" I asked, genuinely curious about how people drank that crap. I guess I hadn't noticed the flavor when I put it away last night.

"Oh, you're gonna give me shit for liking pumpkin spice too? My bestie, Lexi, is always giving me a hard time about it," she huffed. "I'm a basic bitch, okay? It's not my fault that it's the perfect fall flavor."

I placed the cup of coffee and the creamer on the island as she took a seat. "I'm not saying anything." I raised my hands in surrender.

Daphne took a deep breath. "So, about last night," she started, her eyes avoiding mine, "I, um, I don't usually do things like that. I mean, sleeping around. I just barged in here and messed up your solo trip, so I'm gonna get out of your hair this morning and go find a place to stay in town." She nervously picked at her mug. It was cute that she was a little off-balance around me, but I had to try to make her more comfortable. I needed to figure out how to get her to stay.

"Hey, there's no rush, and I hope you don't think I do stuff like this all the time either. You were definitely an unexpected but very welcome surprise." I winked.

Oh God, what was I doing?

I think she may have actually cringed at me. "Yeah, but last night was a mistake. We both came here to get over exes and clear our heads, and instead, we numbed our pain with each other. While I had a great time, I don't think it was the best idea I've ever had. After I've had my coffee, I'll get out of here." She shook her head as if she was trying to get the images from last night out of there.

She was right, of course, but the fact remained that I had no regrets about getting lost in her last night. "I had a great time too, and I totally get where you're coming from, but you don't have to go. I know this is a strange situation, but there's plenty of room, and I promise to be on my very best behavior—no more losing control. Maybe we can even have some fun. Platonic fun, of course, while we try to forget about our crappy relationships." She was staring at me as if I had lost my mind again, but she hadn't said no yet, so I continued. "I'll be busy writing anyway. You'll have plenty of time to yourself, to relax, to explore the town, and then when you want some company, maybe we can share a meal or something."

"I think it's called a one-night stand for a reason. You don't usually see each other a second time, let alone live with them for a week. This is weird, right? I mean, I'll admit that last night was pretty amazing, but it was a one-time thing. I'm not trying to get involved with someone so soon." She was making total sense, but I wasn't having any of it.

"I couldn't agree more, but, like you said last night, you still need to get your money back from this mix-up with the rental, and I'm happy to share the cabin while we figure it out. It's a weird situation for sure, but we're both adults. Surely, we can share the same space without jumping on each other again." I chuckled. I believed not one word of what was coming out of my mouth, but if it made her stay, I'd do and say just about anything at this point. I'd even keep it in the friend zone, for now.

She sat quietly for a moment and stared into her now-empty coffee mug. I was sure she'd say no. I reached for her mug to refill it and she looked up at me. When her eyes met mine, I knew this girl could absolutely ruin me, and I was going to let her. Pulling me out of my thoughts, she said,

"Okay." I blinked. Did she just agree to stay? "I'll stay for now, but if shit gets weird, well, any weirder, I'm outta here."

10

DAPHNE

After that awkward chat in the kitchen this morning, Nathan went to shower and get ready for the day, so I took the opportunity to call Lexi and fill her in on everything that had happened. She, of course, was over the moon and couldn't wait for us to have a round two. I assured her that would not be happening, but she wasn't hearing any of it. In fact, she was convinced that this was exactly what would help me get over Marcus and all of his bullshit. I believe her exact words were something along the lines of, "You can spend the week fucking that asshole out of your system."

Well, that wasn't on my agenda and I was looking forward to spending the week avoiding Nathan like the plague. The man appeared way too perfect to be real, and the last thing I needed was to get attached to yet another man who would ultimately disappoint me. My heart was just starting to feel lighter after only being away from

Marcus for a few days. His type of "love" took a toll on my heart, and I didn't need to be thinking about getting mixed up with someone new.

When I hung up with Lexi, I showered and got dressed in a thick flannel top with a pair of my favorite jeans and comfy booties, my basic bitch uniform, if you will. I was excited to go out and explore the town. This place was a fall lover's dream, and I was determined to enjoy every single minute of my time here.

My stomach growled, making me realize I hadn't eaten anything since the popcorn during the movie last night and it was now almost noon. The popcorn. The kissing. The chemistry. The orgasms. Nope, nope, nope. I had to stop thinking about last night. Maybe a walk around town would help clear my head.

As I emerged from my bedroom and entered the living area, I spotted Nathan set up at the dining table, tapping away on his laptop. He looked up at me over his glasses as I approached, and good God, did he look good. I had to get it together. I had to get out of there. "Hey, I'm gonna go check out the town and grab a bite to eat. I'll see you later, I guess," I said as I turned and walked to the door.

I heard the scrape of a chair across the wood floor and turned to see Nathan stand and ask, "Mind if I join you?" Um, yes, sir, I would mind that very much. "I'm starving, and I could use a break." Shit. How do I say no? I guess it wouldn't kill me to have lunch with him. Would it?

"Um, okay." I seemed unsure because I was. This wasn't what I imagined when he said I'd have plenty of alone time, but I also wasn't an asshole, and I wasn't about to deny the man a meal. He disappeared into his room and came back wearing a long-sleeve Henley that looked like it was painted onto his damn skin and a pair of jeans that fit him perfectly.

This mother fucker.

He insisted on driving, and I let him because I wanted to take in the scenery in the daylight. I had gotten to the cabin at dusk, but now I could fully appreciate the changing leaves and cute cottages that lined the road that wound past the lake. It looked like it was straight out of one of those cheesy fall Hallmark movies—I loved it. I spent the drive taking in the scenery and snapping pictures with my phone, so we hadn't made much conversation. When we parked on Main Street, Nathan jumped out of the car so fast that I had barely leaned down to grab my bag off the floor when he was already opening the passenger door for me. "Oh, thanks," I said as I gawked up at him with furrowed brows. He was being awfully chivalrous for someone who said we were going to be keeping things platonic.

Main Street was exactly as I had imagined it would be, with a typical cozy small-town feel. Mature trees lined the street, and their fallen leaves littered the sidewalks. There were several small shops, a market, a café, and a bookshop. Yes, please! The town was so picturesque. It was easy to see why this was a popular destination for social media influencers, but I was thankful that it wasn't a zoo. It would totally ruin the vibes if it were overrun by people snapping selfies all over.

We made our way into the cute diner on the corner from

where we parked. Walking in was like stepping back in time. It looked as if it had been recently restored to its original glory, and I appreciated that they didn't try to modernize the decor. It was perfect and reminded me of my favorite diner in the city, where Lexi and I frequented. I was admiring my surroundings when we were greeted by a friendly, older woman with a warm smile, who held menus and directed us to a booth by the windows.

Nathan and I were silent as we perused the menus. I was still avoiding his gaze. Why did he make me so nervous? Prior to Marcus, I had been a confident woman. I was playful, a smartass. My time with Marcus had changed me. I didn't realize what had happened until it was too late. I had become docile and accommodating, avoiding confrontation at all costs, trying not to "wake the beast," as it were. Marcus never hit me or became violent toward me, but he didn't have to. His mood swings were chaotic, and I thought they were my fault. I did everything I could to keep him happy to avoid them. I know now I wasn't responsible for his moods or how he treated me, but you don't get over shit like that overnight, and Marcus wasn't giving me the time or space to do that. Since I'd been gone, Marcus had called a few times and sent a few texts, all of which echoed the same theme—he was sorry and I needed to come home so we could work things out. He seemed genuine in his messages, but I knew better. I was all too familiar with his brand of manipulation.

"What are you having?" Nathan pulled me back into the

present. "I'm starving." He was looking at me as if he wanted to eat me. Or was that wishful thinking?

No, Daphne, down girl.

"Mmm, me too. Probably a grilled cheese and soup. I'm a sucker for a good grilled cheese. I have to at least try them everywhere I go, especially if they look like this." I pointed to the picture in the menu as I licked my lips to make sure I didn't drool on the table.

"Oh, that does look good," he agreed as the waitress came back and took our orders.

Nathan and I fell into easy conversation. We talked about our families, our childhoods, and what we did for work. There weren't any extended silences unless our mouths were full of food, which was delicious. It was comfortable and easy. The awkwardness from this morning was gone.

Nathan leaned back in the booth. "So, tell me more about being an ICU nurse. What made you get into that? Seems like a stressful job."

"Yeah, it can be stressful and sometimes sad, but it's also super rewarding. When a particularly sick patient makes it out of there and comes back to say 'thank you'… there's nothing like that in the world." Shit, I was tearing up. "Sorry." I wiped a napkin under my eye.

Nathan reached a hand across the table and rested it on my arm. "There's nothing to be sorry for. You care, and that's why you are probably a great nurse. Your patients and their families are lucky to have you caring for them."

"Thanks, I appreciate that. But to answer your other

question, I don't have some grand, selfless story of why I got into it. I wanted job security, and the sight of blood didn't bother me," I laughed. "I know it's not the reason most people expect, but it's the truth. But it turns out I absolutely love what I do and I couldn't imagine doing anything else."

"Hey, there's no shame in doing something because it pays the bills, but you're lucky to also love what you do." Nathan's hand still rested on my arm, and he gave me a squeeze. "I have so much respect for nurses." His eyes closed, and I could almost feel his pain as he continued, "My mom passed away a few years back, and the nurses were the true heroes whenever she was in and out of the hospital. Don't get me wrong, most people were helpful and kind, but her nurses were absolutely amazing."

"Oh, Nathan, I'm so sorry. I can only imagine how difficult that must have been." I placed my hand over his and gave him a squeeze.

"Thank you. It was hard for all of us, but no one more than my dad. She was the love of his life." He seemed to drift off into a memory. "But I'm glad they had the time they did together. They give me hope for the future." He paused, then pulled his arm back. "Okay, enough sad shit, let's go explore the rest of the town."

After we finished up and Nathan paid, despite my protests, we headed out to walk along Main Street. I was eager to explore the town, and Nathan being here wasn't going to stop me. There were quite a few more people out now than had been before we went into the diner. Couples strolled hand in hand, friends laughed, and families took in the sights. It truly was like a scene from a movie.

We passed several storefronts, stopping briefly here and there to window shop. Occasionally, I'd feel Nathan's hand on the small of my back, guiding me through the crowded parts of the sidewalk. I did my best to remain unaffected by him, but it was almost impossible. He was so charming and easy to be around, and every time he touched me, he set my skin on fire. This week was going to be harder than I thought.

Maybe I should still investigate some accommodation options?

I spotted the bookshop a few doors down and grabbed Nathan's hand, apparently forgetting what his touch did to me, and started to drag him toward it. "Daphne, what are you…" He started as I clearly caught him off guard. He squeezed my hand and planted his feet. "Ah, maybe that's not the best idea." His sudden worried expression confused me.

"Why? Afraid too many adoring fans will accost you?' I teased. He swallowed. "Wait, are you famous or something? What's your pen name?"

"N.J. Pierce."

Holy fucking shit. I hadn't thought much of it when he said he was a romance author—I mean, isn't everyone these days? I also hadn't thought to ask if I might have read anything that he'd written. Because what were the odds, right? And when we talked about his work, he didn't mention anything that would lead me to believe that he was a well-known, bestselling author.

Fuck me.

I had, in fact, heard of him. I even had a few of his books on my TBR, but I hadn't read anything from him yet, and I most definitely had no idea what he looked like. I attempted to regain my composure and not fangirl like an idiot. "Oh, shit." I failed.

He laughed and pulled me closer. I was still holding his hand, and the act looked and felt more intimate than I'm sure he meant it. "Hey, I'm just me. It'll be fine. Let's go in." His eyes searched mine. He said it so casually, like we'd known each other forever. I was looking up at him, blinking, and I swear that if he had tried to kiss me again at that moment, I would've happily let him. Instead, he started walking to the bookshop with my hand still in his.

Nathan opened the door to the bookshop and guided me in with his hand on the small of my back again. Those small gestures fed my romance-starved heart. I couldn't remember the last time Marcus had done anything like that, or if he ever did.

11

NATHAN

Walking into The Cozy Quill—*cute name, by the way*—my focus was on Daphne as she took in our surroundings. The bookshop was exactly as one might expect to find in a quaint small town. It was clean and tidy, but looked as if it hadn't been updated in a long time. The book stacks were in tight, neatly organized rows. There was mismatched furniture items set up near the front where one could sit and read. The shop smelled of books and something earthy with a hint of citrus. It was amazing. I loved old bookshops and, by the look on Daphne's face, so did she.

Behind the counter was a small woman with graying hair, wearing what looked to be a homemade cardigan. She looked up through her wire-rimmed glasses and smiled as we entered. "Can I help you find anything, dears?"

"Thanks, but I think we're just browsing," I said in reply.

"No worries. I'm Myrtle. Just holler if you need anything," she offered casually and then returned her attention to the book on the counter in front of her.

Daphne turned to me with a smile on her face that made me feel things I had no business feeling. She was sunshine. She was breathtaking. She was so much more than I had expected. "This place is amazing," she whispered as we made our way through the stacks. I watched her run her fingers over the shelves, taking everything in. "Do you think they stock your books here? We should see if you can sign some and surprise your readers!" That wasn't something I had done before, and it wasn't something I'd ordinarily do, but she seemed so excited at the prospect, how could I refuse? We made our way to the romance section and saw that there were a few of my books on the shelf.

After checking to make sure it was okay with Myrtle, I rejoined Daphne in the romance section. I found her sitting on the floor with her legs crisscrossed and my latest novel open in her lap. She was bent over toward the book, but I could see her blushing cheeks. I cleared my throat as I approached, and she quickly shut the book. *Adorable.*

I spent the next few minutes signing books and handing them back to Daphne to re-shelf for me. We were so close, almost touching, and when our hands grazed one another, a chill ran through my body. I was immediately brought back to last night and how good it felt when she fell apart in my arms. "This is so cool," Daphne said excitedly as we worked to straighten out the shelves we had disturbed. "I can't believe you're a famous author."

I chuckled. I guess I was, but only in certain circles. For example, Daphne had heard of me but didn't recognize me. That was usually the case unless I was at some sort of signing event. The only other time I had been recognized in public was when I was at a bookstore, so I usually avoided the romance sections to be safe. It's not that I didn't love my fans, because I did, but the attention made me uncomfortable for some reason. I'd always been a pretty private person, and I was still getting used to being in the spotlight.

I reached my hand out for Daphne to help her up from the floor, and she accepted it. We browsed around for a few more minutes before I noticed she was still carrying my most recent novel. "What are you doing with that?" I raised an eyebrow and gestured to the book.

"Buying it." She beamed. "I'm excited to read something you've written. And besides, I could use a new book, anyway." We headed to the front to pay for the book, where we were greeted by Myrtle and her fluffy cat, who stood at attention on the counter, demanding to be pet. Daphne was fussing over the fluffy beast while I coaxed the book from her hand and paid for it. "What are you doing?" she asked as she pulled herself away from her new feline friend.

"My treat," I said and handed my credit card over to Myrtle.

"You didn't have to do that, but thank you." Daphne squeezed my forearm and then stepped back to snuggle the cat some more.

Myrtle rang me up and thanked us for coming in and signing the books. "The local ladies will be thrilled. Wait until I tell the book club!" She beamed, "You're welcome back any time, and if you happen back into town, please let me know. I'd love to set something up for you here in the shop."

"You're too kind, and I'd love to. If I end up back here again, I'll be sure to stop in." We waved our goodbyes and headed out of the shop. "Thanks for letting me tag along with you today. I know you didn't plan for the company. I hope it wasn't too much of an inconvenience."

"You know, today was a lot of fun. I'm glad that I had you for company." She leaned into me for a side hug, and I took that opportunity to put my lips to the top of her head and breathe her in. Was that vanilla? She smelled so good, and I again found myself daydreaming about last night. There was no way I was going to be able to keep this girl in the friend zone. "Do we need anything from the store before we head back to the cabin?" She looked up at me through her lashes, still tucked into my side.

"Yeah, let's go get some supplies." I smiled down at her as she stepped away from me, and I immediately felt the loss of her body next to mine. We walked a few more doors down and into a small grocery store to grab some essentials and replace Daphne's broken wine bottle with several others.

"Let's try not to break these when we get home, okay?" I joked as we walked back to the car.

"Listen, you keep your clothes on and maybe we won't have a problem. Your naked chest was very shocking," she laughed as she bumped into my side.

"Hey, you barged in on my solo getaway, remember? If I had known I was having company, maybe I would have put on a shirt," I chuckled as we loaded up the car. I opened her door and helped her in because my momma raised me to be a gentleman. When I did things like that, though, she looked at me strangely. It was as if she didn't know what it felt like to be treated with respect and kindness. *What a shame.* She deserved that and so much more.

We started off to the cabin and fell back into effortless conversation. When we were halfway back to the house, she pulled out her phone to look at an incoming text. Her brows furrowed, and her jaw clenched. "What's the matter?" I asked.

"Nothing," she said as she shoved her phone back in her bag, her mouth pressed into a thin line.

"Are you sure? It looks like something's the matter." I raised an eyebrow at her. She was clearly upset, and I had an overwhelming urge to find out why, so I could fix it.

She huffed and rolled her eyes. "It's just my ex. He's been relentless since I left. I'm fine, really. I don't want to talk about him."

12

DAPHNE

Fucking Marcus. Seriously, fuck him. It had taken me months to build up the confidence to leave him finally, and now he won't leave me alone. Nathan and I had a great day exploring the town. Our friendship, or whatever the hell it was, was so light and fun. I don't think I'd smiled that much in months, maybe in years. I truly had the best time. I had even temporarily forgotten about Marcus and my mess of a life.

When we got back to the cabin, we went to our separate rooms. I hated to admit it, but hearing from Marcus again had shaken me, and my head was all over the place. I knew Marcus was a dickhead, but his messages were messing with my mind and I was, suddenly, exhausted.

I must have fallen asleep because some time later, I was in bed, waking up to the sun setting.

Oopsie.

I rubbed the sleep out of my eyes and stretched. The

smell of something delicious drew me out of bed and to the kitchen.

Does this freaking man cook too? Goddammit.

When I emerged from the bedroom, the broad lines of Nathan's back greeted me. Nathan's *naked* back. He was facing away from me, tending to something on the stove, so I took the opportunity to truly appreciate his form. My eyes traveled from his strong, muscular shoulders and back, down his tapered waist, and landed longingly on his tight ass, cloaked in yet another pair of goddamned gray sweatpants. I was staring at his ass like I was starving and he was going to be my last meal. I think I may have been drooling when I heard his throat clear. My eyes shot up to his.

Busted.

"Excuse me, ma'am, but my eyes are up here," he said with a smirk as he pointed two fingers at his eyes.

I covered my face with my hands. "Oh my God, stop it," I snorted. "But seriously, didn't we *just* have this conversation? Where's your freaking shirt?" I pointed at his naked chest.

He laughed. God, that laugh. "Oh, I'm sorry, so it's my fault that you were ogling me? You know I'm not a piece of meat, Daphne."

"I was *not* ogling you!" My cheeks flamed with embarrassment.

"Okay, okay, you know I'm just messing with you. I'll go cover myself so you can stop malfunctioning," he chuckled as he headed off to his room. I circled the island to get myself a glass of water. I was guzzling down my second glass when Nathan reappeared, wearing yet another fitted tee that did nothing to hide the shape of him.

Great.

I did my best to compose myself. Unfortunately, my best wasn't good enough, and I kept thinking about last night. I don't know if I've ever come that hard or that many times with any other partner, and I wanted a repeat. Even thinking about it was a mistake, though. I wasn't ready for a relationship, and I knew without a shadow of a doubt that I could fall hard and fast for this guy if I weren't careful. *Get it together, Daphne.* "So whatcha making?"

"Hope you're hungry. I'm making chicken parm—it's my mom's recipe." *Fuck, fuck, fuck.* Italian food was my love language.

"Oh, that sounds good, and it smells amazing!" I sat at the island while Nathan opened a bottle of wine. He poured two glasses and offered me one that I gratefully accepted.

He turned back to his task at hand. "So, is everything okay? You looked upset before you disappeared earlier."

"Yeah, I'm okay. My ex is making me question my sanity at the moment," I confessed. *Why was he so easy to talk to?* I wouldn't ordinarily confide these feelings to a stranger. "That was his MO throughout our entire relationship. He gaslit the shit out of me and made me think I was wrong, or that I was going crazy. It's exhausting."

"Shit, I'm so sorry, Daphne." He turned to look at me with a sad smile.

I didn't want his pity and I sure as shit didn't need to be pouring my heart out to him. Sure, we shared a night of hot as fuck sex, but he was still basically a stranger, and I had to remember that. "It's fine, really. I don't want to talk about it," I said as I gulped down a healthy serving of my wine. "Let's talk about something else. Did you get any work done today after we got back?"

He eyed me as if he wanted to pry a little more, but thankfully dropped it. "Yeah, a little. I was a little distracted myself." His face twisted. "Seems my ex saw a picture of us in town together today, and she was less than thrilled."

My jaw dropped, and I blinked rapidly. "Um, what in the fresh hell? How? When? Who?" I stammered over my words and then took another gulp of wine.

His hand tugged on the back of his neck as he grimaced, "Yeah, so I guess someone recognized me in town and snapped a pic of us. They posted it to their socials and tagged me. Courtney saw it and kind of freaked out."

I quickly pulled out my phone and searched for him online. Yep, there it was, a photo of us looking like we were fucking together. It was taken moments before we entered the bookshop, and it looked like an intimate moment between lovers.

"Well, that doesn't look good," I winced. "But why is she so mad? I thought she cheated on you, and that's why you ended things. I don't think she's got much room to talk."

"She's upset because she thinks I moved on too quickly. Whatever. I didn't respond to her. I know it's probably not the most mature reaction, but I don't owe her an explanation."

Just then, my phone chimed with an incoming message. "Looks like the cat's outta the bag on my end too," I laughed as I read the incoming message from Lexi.

LEXI

Bitch—have you seen this???

She attached a screenshot of the social media post we were just talking about. I ignored the message. I didn't want to deal with it right now.

"Lexi sent that pic to me too. I guess it's getting around." I took another long pull from my wine glass as Nathan rounded the island to top off my drink.

I set my glass down, put my forehead on the island, and groaned. I hadn't told my parents Marcus, and I had broken up yet. They were gonna freak if they saw this. I was hoping for a fun little solo vacay to relax before dealing with that conversation. My parents loved Marcus, or at least they loved the version of him he presented to them. I hadn't confided in them how bad things had gotten. The truth was, I was embarrassed that I had let it go on for as long as I did.

I exhaled a long breath and looked up at a concerned Nathan, who was next to me now with his hand resting on my back. I blinked away the moisture gathering in my eyes. *Fuck, why was I so emotional?* It all felt like too much. I just wanted more time before talking to my parents and seeing the disappointment in their eyes. I knew I was right to leave him, but explaining why I left and how long I stayed with him despite those reasons felt overwhelming.

"It's going to be okay," Nathan said as he slowly rubbed my back, calming me slightly.

"I know, but I haven't even told my parents about Marcus and me…I thought it could wait until I got home." *Home.* Shit, I still didn't have a home when I got back. "Ya know what? It's going to be fine, and I'm not dealing with this now," I laughed. Humor was my go-to coping mechanism, and while this wasn't exactly funny, it was a laugh-or-cry situation, and I'll be damned if I was going to turn into a puddle in front of this man.

Warily, Nathan started back toward the stove. "Okay, if you don't want to talk about it, that's fine. But just know we're in this together now, so if you do want to talk or need anything, I'm here for you." *Swoon.* Nathan was so understanding and easy-going. I felt as though I could talk to him and tell him why I was upset, but I was still being cautious.

"I appreciate that. I do. I want to live in avoidance for a bit longer, if that's all right?" I chuckled. "But I'm starving, and I cannot wait to dig into this. It smells so freaking good."

"Want to eat by the fire? We can throw on another scary movie if you want to," he said as he plated our dinner.

"That sounds great, actually. Scary movies *and* Italian food? Be still, my heart," I joked while clutching my chest as I turned to the living room. "I'll find something to put on."

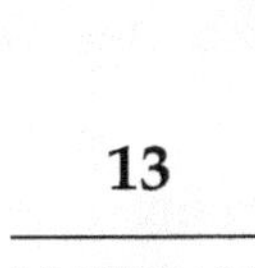

13

NATHAN

I watched her walk away, and my eyes roamed down over her body. I couldn't help myself. She was beautiful, but it wasn't just that. We'd had the best day together—conversation had flowed freely. She was fun and funny as hell. Her fantastic ass was the icing on the cake, and I couldn't stop thinking about how good it felt while I was gripping it last night as I drove into her again and again. I shook my head. I had to try to keep my thoughts platonic. She didn't, no more accurately, we didn't need the complications, especially not right now.

I finished plating our dinner, complete with crispy garlic bread from the oven. The scent immediately brought me back to my childhood. This was always my mom's favorite thing to make, and I used to love to cook with her when I was younger. Pulling me out of my memories, Daphne returned to the kitchen to retrieve the wine and our glasses.

"I've got the booze," she said as she made her way back to the living room.

"On my way," I called after her as I gathered our plates and utensils. When I entered the living room, the fire was crackling, the lights were dimmed, and cushions were splayed out on the floor around the coffee table. The area had been cozy and welcoming when we arrived, but now it had been transformed into an intimate dinner setting. I smiled. "This looks great, Daphne. What are we watching?"

"Halloween?" she said in a question, seeking my approval.

"Sounds great." Truth be told, I didn't care what we watched. I was looking forward to hanging out with her some more. We settled into our seats, and Daphne started the movie while I passed her a plate.

"Nathan, this looks amazing! Thank you so much for cooking. I really appreciate this."

"No need to thank me. It's my pleasure. I enjoy cooking. I used to cook with my mom all the time when I was younger," I reminisced.

Daphne raised her glass toward me. "Well, I'm very thankful for that right now. Cheers!"

"Cheers." I raised my glass to her. I watched with anticipation as Daphne dug into her meal.

"Mmmmm," she practically moaned. "This is delicious." It was hard not to imagine the sounds she had made last night, which sounded much the same as the sounds she was making with each bite. I adjusted myself discreetly under the table. Fuck, this was going to be harder than I thought, pun intended.

"Daphne, if you keep making noises like that, our 'platonic' status will be in serious jeopardy," I joked.

Daphne choked on her garlic bread, and that did nothing to dissuade the growing situation in my pants. I chuckled. She coughed and her cheeks pinkened as she attempted to regain her composure. She was so fucking adorable. "You okay?"

"Yep." She popped the P. "Just went down the wrong pipe," she said, then coughed. It was cute that she thought I'd buy that. We continued eating and making small talk while watching the movie. Turns out Daphne was a huge horror movie fan. Last night, things were too sexually charged to find that out. Even though I could tell she knew this movie by heart, she still jumped and screamed at the jump scares on the screen.

Cute.

When we had finished eating, Daphne got up and grabbed the plates, despite my objections, and took them into the kitchen. I followed her and opened another bottle of wine since we had already finished the first one. Daphne loaded the dishes into the dishwasher. I had already taken care of the pots and pans I had used to cook because my mom had taught me to clean as I went. I was very grateful for that advice because I was eager to get back to the movie and, more importantly, the company I was watching it with.

Back in the living room, Daphne and I both sat on the couch, not close enough to touch, but not on opposite ends either. We shared a cozy blanket and settled in to finish the movie. Much like the night before, I was hard-pressed to keep my eyes on the screen. I was mesmerized by Daphne, watching her reactions and memorizing her features. It surprised me how little I had thought about Courtney since meeting Daphne. Her betrayal hurt, but Daphne lessened that sting a little more with every moment we spent together.

I glanced back at Daphne again as she pulled the blanket up over her mouth and nose. I guess something scary was about to happen on screen. I grinned as she turned to glance at me. *Busted.* She smiled. "What?"

"It's nothing. I just love how into this you are," I said honestly. "I mean, how many times have you seen this movie? Be honest."

"I really couldn't say. A lot?" She laughed, "I love Halloween, fall, and all things spooky season. Horror movies are a staple for me this time of year." With a shrug, she turned back to the movie. I was enchanted with her. She gave off an energy that I found irresistible. I smiled to myself. I wanted her, and not just as a hookup. We fit together and though I knew our timing was shit, I couldn't help the way I felt.

At the next suspenseful scene, as Daphne pulled the blanket nearly up to her eyes, I moved in slightly closer to her. She wasn't paying me any attention, so I took that opportunity to drape my arm behind her on the back of the couch. I wasn't trying to be a creep, but I had this over-whelming desire to be closer to her. I wanted to feel the warmth of her body against mine. I needed it. Then, when she jumped at what was happening on the screen, I moved my arm that was behind her slightly until my hand pressed into her shoulder, and when she leaned into me, I breathed out a sigh and pulled her closer.

"Platonic, huh?" She smirked up at me from the crook of my arm.

"Fuck platonic," I growled as I leaned down further into her personal space. Her breath hitched as her eyes bounced between mine and then to my mouth. Her tongue darted out to wet her lips.

Hell yes.

Our mouths met in a fury, tongues lashing, teeth nipping. One hand was gripping the back of her head, tangled in her hair. My other hand gripped her waist and pulled her to me. Her hands were clawing at my shirt and pulling me in closer still. Our breaths were labored, our movements frantic.

Then she laid her hands flat on my chest and pushed me back. "Wait," she gasped, "what are we doing?" Her chest heaved as she stared back at me, waiting for me to come to my senses. The thing was, I had lost all sense of self-preservation, and all I could see was her. In that moment, I could so clearly see a life with her. I knew it was crazy. We had only just met, but it was as if we were supposed to meet. I had never been a believer in fate or shit like that, but I felt it with her. This couldn't be a coincidence, could it?

I studied her as I chose my next words. What *were* we doing? What did I want? Would she be open to it? Do I lie and tell her this means nothing or risk scaring her away with the truth? Fuck me.

"Truthfully? I don't know, but I want more than platonic. I want you, whatever you're willing to give." Our breaths were still ragged. Her eyes searched my face and then closed as she exhaled a deep breath.

"Fuck it," she whispered, and when she opened her eyes again, there was a renewed fire there. It was so on. I didn't know what it meant for the future, but at that moment, I didn't care. We'd figure it out later.

Simultaneously, we attacked one another. My mouth was on hers. Her lips parted to grant me access. I could taste the wine on her as I deepened our kiss. Her hands grabbed at my shirt as I leaned all the way back onto the couch, pulling her along with me so that she was on top of me. I reached up and wound my hand in her hair while I used my other hand to find one of her tight nipples. She moaned as I swiped my thumb over it.

Her moan made me feral. I grabbed her around the waist, flipped us over, and started tearing at her clothes. I wanted her naked immediately. I pulled her sweatshirt up over her head, and then our mouths met in another passionate kiss that rivaled all the ones that came before. Her hands trailed down and grazed against my growing erection. I was so hard for her, painfully so. I needed more. I pressed into her with my length and she moaned again, "Oh God, Nathan."

"That's right, Baby, I'm your god." Damn it, that may have sounded like a line from one of my books, but this was all us. She had turned me into a filthy-mouthed, pussy-drunk, crazy person, and I loved every second. She pulled down my sweatpants and gripped my length with a rough stroke. I growled, "Fuck, Kitten," as I took her mouth again while pulling at her leggings.

She broke our kiss and pushed me away. At first, I thought she had come to her senses until I realized she was trying to remove her leggings. I stood to give her some room while I stripped out of my clothes. When I removed my sweatpants, my thick cock bobbed between us, drawing her gaze. She was practically drooling at me as she scrambled up onto her knees on the couch.

She took me into her mouth and to the back of her throat without a word. Had I died and gone to heaven? Fuck, her mouth was perfect. Soft and warm and wet. She ran her tongue over the tip while looking me in the eyes and then took me to the back of her throat again. When she gagged, I moaned. Shit, I was so close already. This woman was a fucking dick magician. I usually had more control, but Daphne had me on the edge with only a few flicks of the tongue.

I grabbed her chin and pulled her mouth from my cock with a pop. "My turn." My voice strained as I attempted to maintain control. I pushed her back onto the couch and ran my hands slowly up her legs. As I made my way up further, I leaned down to press gentle kisses along my route. Licking, sucking, and kissing a path to where I wanted to be more than anything. Her legs parted for me, and I continued my path. I couldn't wait to taste her again.

I continued my ascent and when I was right where she wanted me, I paused and took a deep inhale. Her scent was intoxicating, and I wanted to savor this moment. She was squirming and trembling with need. "What is it, Kitten? Need something?" I grinned into her. I wanted to draw this out as long as possible and take my time.

"Please," she whispered. "Please, Nathan, I need you to touch me. I need your mouth on me." This time, she spoke up.

"Good girl." I smiled, then swiped through her center slowly with a flat tongue and was rewarded with her deep moan. Mmm, I loved the noises she made. She was so responsive to me. I licked and sucked and kissed like a man possessed. When I placed a thick finger inside of her, she nearly levitated off the couch. When I added the second, she was done. Her pussy clenched around me as her orgasm came crashing through her. She soaked my face, and I gladly drank down every drop.

I sat back on the couch, admiring her. Her face was flushed, her breathing labored, pussy glistening. She was perfect. I licked my lips as I leaned over her, and when we kissed, it was electrifying—it felt different. This kiss was full of longing and passion and something else.

"Baby, I need to be inside of you now," I murmured into her mouth between kisses. "Condoms still in your purse?" I laughed, remembering how I ran from the bedroom last night like a crazy person to get them.

She chuckled, "No, I moved them. Come on." She pushed on my chest to get me off her. Then she grabbed my hand and pulled me to her room. We were practically running and laughed the whole way. When we got inside, she pushed me down on the bed and made her way into the en suite. I sat with my back against the headboard, stroking myself in anticipation. She retrieved the condoms and returned to join me on the bed, ready with one already unwrapped. She threw the rest of them onto the nightstand. "We are gonna need those later," she laughed as she winked at me.

Game on, woman. Game on.

She moved quickly and brushed my hand off my cock, replaced it with her own, and then took me to the back of her throat again. I pressed up to meet her and made her gag. Holy hell, that was one of the sexiest sounds on the planet. She removed me from her mouth with a sly smile and then proceeded to roll the condom onto me. As soon as it was in place, I lost what was left of my already dwindling control, grabbed her, and spun us so that her back was on the bed. She squealed and then laughed again. Her laugh was music to my ears. I reached behind her head and intertwined my fingers in her hair, pulling her into me almost violently. Our mouths crashed together as I entered her in one swift motion.

"Holy fuck," she practically shouted. She was dripping for me and ready, but still surprised by the intrusion.

"Yeah, Baby, that's right. Scream for me," I said as I thrust into her again and again. I continued to kiss her mouth and her neck, moving down to take one of her stiff nipples into my mouth while toying with the other. She was meeting my every thrust and moaning my name, and as I reached between us and pressed on her clit, she exploded. Again, there was a rush of wetness as her pussy pulsed around me. I continued moving in long, deep thrusts, slowing slightly as she came down from one orgasm and into another.

When she had come down from yet another orgasm, I flipped us while still connected and drove up into her, hitting her from a different angle, earning me yet another deep moan. She sat up and rode me slowly, her eyes meeting mine, full of emotion. *Could she feel it too?* I hoped I wasn't alone in my feelings for her. I continued to stroke her swollen bundle of nerves as she increased her speed, grinding against me.

I was spellbound. The curve of her hips, the swell of her breasts, her parted lips, the sweat dripping down her neck to roll down between her perfect tits. I was so close. I wanted this to last, but she was gripping me so tight I was going to burst at any moment, so I pulled her down to me. I kissed her while slowly driving up into her, controlling our tempo.

After another thrust, she came hard around me, and that did me in. My motions became erratic as I came. I continued to fuck her slowly through our orgasms. When she stopped pulsing around me, we just lay there. Her with her head on my chest and me with my arms wrapped around her, holding her and stroking her back gently.

Daphne broke the silence first. "Wow." *Wow was fucking right.* That was amazing.

I grinned into her hair. "Wow is right," I agreed. "Amazing, even."

She laughed and sat up to look at me. "Well, I guess I'd better go get cleaned up." She looked around nervously, not as confident as she had been while she was riding me, taking what she wanted. I was still inside her, and she was nervous. Interesting.

"Come on," I urged her as I started to get up.

She looked confused, "What are you…" she yelped when I picked her up and tossed her over my shoulder, and then started walking out of the room. "Oh shit. Nathan, what are you doing?" she screeched.

Chuckling, I kept walking and smacked her ass. "We're gonna get cleaned up."

14

DAPHNE

Holy hell that was so freaking hot. The chemistry between Nathan and me was undeniable, but our connection felt much deeper than just sex, and that was absolutely terrifying. I wasn't ready. I was still reeling from my relationship with dickhead. There was no way I was in the right headspace to start something new. Yet there I was, being carried across the cabin and into a spacious en suite by this beautiful man.

With me still resting over his shoulder, he reached into the giant walk-in shower to turn it on and adjust the temperature. He set me down to retrieve a couple of fluffy towels from a small linen closet before returning with a sexy grin. His gaze was hungry as he stalked back to me. I was completely caught off guard as he swept me up into his arms and attacked my mouth with another hungry kiss. My ass slammed onto the vanity as he set me down and continued his assault. Hot, wet kisses trailed down my neck and chest. His hands were everywhere, kneading and pawing my breasts and ass. Nathan flicked a tongue over my nipple and I cried out.

It was as if he knew exactly what to do to get me off and fast. I was panting and moaning and so close to another orgasm, and he wasn't even touching me where I needed him most. My clit was aching, my pussy clenching at nothing. It was almost unbearable. I reached between us to stroke his thickening length, earning me an animalistic groan. "Aw, does Kitten want more?" He smiled against my chest.

"Yes, Nathan, please," I begged, and with my next breath, I was being lifted again. Nathan slammed us into the wall of the shower with his muscular arms, protecting me from any harm, warm water spraying over us both. Our kisses were frantic, my legs wrapped around his narrow waist. I could feel his thick cock grinding against my dripping pussy. "Nathan, fuck me, please," I pleaded.

Nathan pulled back to look at me, and the desire I saw in his eyes took my breath away. "Shit, I left the condoms."

"Fuck the condoms," I said, surprising myself. Marcus and I always used condoms, and I was on the pill. Nathan had just gotten out of a long-term relationship too, so he was probably good too, right? My vagina clearly didn't give a shit, and that bitch was evidently running the show. Nathan was breathing heavily and looked torn. "I'm all clear, and I'm on the pill."

"I'm good too," he rushed out. "After Courtney cheated

on me, I got tested just to be sure, and we haven't been intimate since. You sure?"

"Fuck yes." And with that, he repositioned himself and thrust into me bare. Holy fucking shit. He fucked me slow and hard while we kissed and touched each other everywhere. His thumb found its way to stroke my already sensitive clit, and I shattered around him again. "Oh, fuck, Nathan, yes, that feels so fucking good," I encouraged him as he picked up his pace.

"Yeah, Baby? You like that?" he murmured into my neck. "Come for me again." And I did with a scream. "Such a good girl for me, Daphne." Sex had never been like this before. I'd always found it difficult to have an orgasm with my past partners, but Nathan seemed to have discovered the damn roadmap to getting me off and I was fucking here for it.

Nathan fucked me mercilessly through several more orgasms and for what seemed like forever. Was it minutes or hours? Who knew? I lost all concept of time until his movements became unsteady and he came inside of me with a roar.

A few moments passed as we both tried to calm our breathing. Nathan kissed me deeply and set me back down on my feet. "You're amazing," he whispered through one last kiss. I smiled up at him and watched him turn to add some body wash to a washcloth. Then this man washed me, like from head to toe, washed me. He took his time, caressing every inch while he cleaned me. That was the sexiest thing I've ever experienced, and I had just been fucked six ways to Sunday by him. But it all felt too intimate, and I had to get the hell out of that shower and back to the safety of my room. Alone.

We had been silent as he washed me and then himself. When he was finished, he turned off the water and wrapped me in a fluffy towel, holding me tightly to him. He kissed the top of my head and then grabbed his own towel and cinched it around his trim waist. Beads of water still dripped down his perfect physique, and I was keenly aware that I was standing there gawking at him. I shook my head. "Um, I'm gonna." I started, motioning with my thumb toward my side of the cabin. But as I turned to leave, his strong hand reached for me and grabbed me by my wrist.

"Stay with me." It wasn't a question.

"I don't think that's a good idea, Nathan," I protested. I was already in danger of falling for this man, and sleeping next to him could very well push me closer to the edge. I stared at where his hand clutched my wrist, then back into his eyes. It would be so easy to fall for him, but I knew better. My heart wasn't ready. I needed time. "Listen, there's no question we have fun together and the sex is amazing, but I'm not ready for more. Please respect that." He nodded, his lips pressed into a thin line, and released my wrist.

I turned and walked quietly back to my room, stopping briefly in the living room to gather my clothes. Reaching my room, I closed the door and pressed my back against it. Closing my eyes, I took a deep breath and recounted the last few hours. I could feel things brewing in my chest despite my efforts to keep my heart out of this.

After a few moments, I dressed in an oversized tee, grabbed my phone, and flopped onto the bed. I was exhausted, but I had to check in with Lexi.

Unfortunately, I was greeted by several missed calls, a voicemail, and numerous texts from Marcus. Ugh, he was so persistent. But why? Looking back at our relationship, he never seemed happy with me, so why was he so fixated on me now? All of his messages had similar themes. *How could you do this to me? You'll never find someone better than me. It's just a matter of time until you come crawling back.* Typical narcissist. How did I not see it sooner? I could've saved myself so much heartache and time. He had me so fucked up—thinking I was the crazy one. Fucking asshole.

Shaking my head, I swiped out of those messages and found my text thread with Lexi. It was late, but she was a night owl, so I'm sure she was still up.

ME

Mayday, mayday

Her reply came almost immediately.

LEXI

What up, hoe?

ME

Oops, I did it again 😣

LEXI

I hope IT is that beautiful man you're shacked up with. 🥒😂

ME

We are not shacked up, but yes we fucked again and yes it was amazing again. I need to get the hell out of here.

LEXI

This is awesome! This is exactly what you needed. I don't get what the issue is.

ME

The issue is I like him. Like, I really like him and I'm not ready.

LEXI

Shut that shit down. There's no reason for feelings to get involved here. Take what you need sexually and bounce.

ME

That's easier said than done for me and you know it.

LEXI

I know—you're my feelings friend 🐱 but lock that shit down. Like you said, you're not ready. Wait—is he interested in more?

ME

Idk honestly. He said he doesn't want platonic, but wasn't clear on where we stand either. Although I didn't give him much of a chance since I basically ran back to my room after.

LEXI

Atta girl—fuck and run. 🐾🐾🐾

ME

You're ridiculous, but I love you. I'm gonna pass out. I'll talk to you tomorrow.

LEXI

Love you too, boo. Oh bt dubs—I packed you another little surprise in the interior pocket of your duffle. You're welcome. 😏

ME

Sweet baby Cheesus. What did you do?

I tossed my phone aside and buried my face in the bed. I loved Lexi, but we were so different. I was a serial relationship person, and she was the queen of the one-night stand. She swore she'd never settle down, and when I was single, I was usually on the hunt for my next Mr. Forever. So far, it hadn't worked out so well for me. I lost myself the last few years being wrapped up in Marcus's bullshit, and now I wanted to work on myself. The last thing I needed was to go and fall in love with my temporary roomie.

Curiosity got the best of me and I pulled myself up off the bed to see what surprise Lexi had hidden for me. In the interior zippered pocket of my duffle was a small bundle of black fabric. I pulled it out, and my jaw hit the floor. Was this supposed to be worn? It was just scraps of fabric all connected into what I assumed was some sort of lingerie. Fucking Lexi.

15

NATHAN

I woke up alone again. When I asked her to stay, she practically ran to her room to get away from me. I mean, I get it—we both are fresh out of relationships that didn't end well. She's a little gun-shy right now, but I felt like we were meant to meet here. It was no coincidence, and I hoped she'd let her guard down long enough to see how good we could be together.

After starting a fresh pot of coffee, I headed out for my morning run. I wasn't particularly a fan of running, nor did I love it, but it was how I started most of my days. It helped me wake up and clear my head so that I could be in the right frame of mind to write, and boy, did I have some thoughts to get down today. I had always found inspiration from real-life situations, and since I was basically living in a forced proximity trope right now, I figured I'd better use it to my advantage. The idea popped into my head on the first night I had met Daphne. Our unusual meet-cute in the foyer hallway, the broken wine bottle, her adorable dumbfounded face. It was all too perfect. If only we could find our way to a happily ever after.

Is that what I wanted?

When I returned from my run, Daphne still hadn't emerged from the safety of her room, so I went for a shower. I should have taken a cold one because as soon as my thoughts drifted back to our time in the shower last night, I began stroking myself. The feel of her bare, the sounds she made for me, the way her pussy clenched around me. Fuck, she was so hot, and we were so good together. I was impossibly hard, and my strokes were erratic. I kept pumping and squeezing, imagining my hand was Daphne's wet heat clenching around me. After only a few minutes, I came forcefully all over the shower wall, wishing I was coming inside Daphne again. If we had only met at a better time, when we both weren't so fresh out of long-term relationships, maybe things could be different between us.

I finished showering, cleaned off the shower wall, and then dressed in my usual work-from-home attire of sweatpants and a T-shirt. I made sure to put on the shirt for Daphne's benefit, although I was tempted to go without just to see her reaction. I loved seeing her get flustered around me. It was cute, but I was determined to be on my best behavior today. If I kept making her nervous, there was little chance of me earning her trust.

I made my way into the kitchen to grab my morning coffee, noticing that Daphne's door was still shut. I hoped it was because it was still early and she was still asleep, and not because she was avoiding me. Then I noticed the coffee pot wasn't quite full, and I realized that Daphne must have come out to get her coffee and then retreated to the safety of her room.

Fuck.

Shaking off the sting of her avoidance, I poured myself a cup and went to my makeshift writing setup at the dining table to start my day. I was still technically on a break, so I didn't have any deadlines to worry about, but I got to work checking my emails when one in particular caught my eye. It was a confirmation email for a romantic dinner I had planned for Courtney and me here at the cabin during what was supposed to be our honeymoon. I must have forgotten to cancel it. It was scheduled for a few days from now, and what I should have done was reply to that email to cancel— what I did, though, defied all logic. Didn't I just tell myself I was going to behave, earn Daphne's trust, keep shit in the friend zone? But no, there I was, clicking "confirm reservation" instead of canceling it. Fuck it. If there's something between us and I let her get away without exploring it, I'd regret it. I had three days to move things in a more romantic direction, and then, hopefully, the dinner would seal the deal.

I replied to a few more emails and then got to work brainstorming my new novel about an emotionally unavailable nurse who reluctantly falls for a romance author in a cabin by a lake.

Some time later, I was staring out the window at the beautiful scenery, lost in thought, when I turned at the sound of Daphne's door creaking open. She wore jeans and an off-the-shoulder sweater, but the suitcase rolling behind her had me jumping to my feet. "Where are you going?" I asked in a panic.

"Hey, yeah, so I got that refund from the rental company, so I was gonna see about staying somewhere in town." Her cheeks were flushed as she spoke. "I'll get out of your hair."

"No, please, stay. I don't want you out of my hair," I pleaded. Jeez, I sounded desperate. I had to wrangle in my emotions. "I mean, we're having fun, right? No need to go somewhere else."

"That's the problem. I think we're having too much fun, if you catch my drift, and not to beat a dead horse, but I'm not looking for anything serious." She was right, of course. We both knew that getting into something serious right now was a mistake. The only difference was I didn't give one single solitary fuck anymore.

"Me neither," I lied. "Listen, the timing is shit, but we get along and we definitely have great chemistry. Why not keep it casual and have some fun? Friends with benefits for the rest of our stay and then we go our separate ways?" I couldn't believe the words that were coming out of my mouth. Casual? Not a chance in hell.

She chewed her lip and looked anywhere but at me while she contemplated my proposition. "There have to be ground rules," she started as she peeked up at me through her dark lashes. "No holding hands or cuddling, no sleepovers." She pressed her lips into a thin line while I assumed she was thinking of more rules. "Basically, no romantic stuff."

"Deal." I didn't hesitate. I wanted to see if we had a future together and the only way to do that was to spend more time together, so I was willing to agree to her terms, even if I had no intention of following them.

"Jesus, this is nuts." She pointed a stern finger at me. "Behave."

"Who, me? I'll be the perfect fuck buddy." I crossed my heart. "That's what this is, right? Friends with benefits?"

Daphne rolled her eyes. "Yeah, I guess. This is so weird and not something I'd ever do. You've definitely caught me on an off week."

"I'll take it," I said with a grin. "Now, any other rules for me, Kitten?" I stalked across the room to her.

She took a step back. And another. "W…what are you doing?" she stammered.

"I'm simply honoring our new agreement. Friends with benefits, was it?" I stepped closer to her. "It's time for some of those benefits."

"Oh shit," she whispered and took off toward her room, abandoning her bags.

16

DAPHNE

I screamed as I felt Nathan grab me around my waist and pick me up. I had almost made it to my room too, but now I was being carried like a sack of potatoes back into the kitchen.

What in the actual fuck did I just agree to? I went from packing my shit to leave to agreeing to being fuck buddies? Lexi would be thrilled. Like seriously, she may throw my vagina a party when I get home, balloons and all.

"I haven't had my breakfast yet, Daphne, and I'm starving," Nathan growled as he placed me on the kitchen island and started pulling off my shoes.

"What are you doing?" I shrieked, even though I knew exactly what he was doing.

"Having my breakfast," he said, unbuttoning my pants as I stared back at him blankly. I think I glitched. I couldn't form words, so I covered my face with my hands and lay back on the island. "Good girl, but put your hands down. I want your eyes on me."

I slowly lowered my hands and stared back at him. There was no way this wouldn't end in heartbreak. Nathan Pierce was going to ruin me.

Fuck it, I thought, sitting up to pull my sweater over my head. Almost immediately, Nathan's mouth was on me, licking my chest, his hands reaching behind me to unhook my bra. He took one of my nipples into his mouth and pinched the other, eliciting a moan from me. I was pulling at my pants. I couldn't get them off fast enough, so Nathan backed away slightly to assist me, tugging them, along with my underwear, swiftly down my legs and onto the floor.

"Lean back, Baby, but keep those gorgeous eyes on me," he panted as he pulled me closer to the edge of the cool surface.

He splayed one large hand across my stomach and the other gripped my thigh as my legs parted for him. I was probably dripping onto the counter at this point, and I didn't care. He met my eyes with a smile and then dipped his head to run his tongue through my wet and needy center.

"Hmm, delicious," he hummed. "So ready for me already."

"Oh my God, Nathan." His mouth felt so good. He continued to attack my center, flicking my clit with his tongue, adding one finger and then another inside of me. I cried out and wriggled on the island. Nathan attempted to keep me still, but I was all over the place and completely unhinged as he continued to fuck me with his fingers.

"Damn, Kitten, you're so responsive to me. Do you like it when I eat this pretty pussy?" I could barely form a thought, let alone words, so I moaned. Seemingly satisfied with my response, he dove back between my thighs to suck my sensitive clit into his mouth again while he fucked me hard and fast with two thick fingers. I felt myself on the edge of a powerful orgasm. My breathing was uneven. I felt lightheaded and then, suddenly, I was falling. Throwing my head back, I came so hard that the now familiar gush of my release sprayed my legs, and it most definitely soaked Nathan. He was completely unfazed and continued to lick me through my orgasm. My clit throbbed, my pussy still clenching around his fingers.

"Holy fuck, Nathan," I uttered when my breath returned to normal.

I squealed as Nathan slid me down off the counter, kissed me hard with a mostly closed mouth, spun me toward my room, and gave my ass a slap. "Now, go get cleaned up while I make you something to eat."

Stunned, I turned my head to look at him with my eyes wide and my mouth agape. What the fuck just happened? I arched an eyebrow. "Yes, sir," I offered with a salute.

"Oh, I like that," he said with a wink and a wide smile.

Grinning to myself, I made my way to my room to get cleaned up, wheeling my suitcase behind me. That was so fucking hot, him taking me on the counter, eating me out like a man possessed, and then sending me on my way. I couldn't stop smiling as I took a quick shower and dressed in leggings and an oversized hoodie.

When I opened my door to head back into the kitchen, the smell of bacon greeted me. *Mmm, bacon.* "Smells good," I said as I entered the kitchen. Nathan turned to face me as I walked in, his hazel eyes and scruffy face, and that devilish grin making my still sensitive clit pulse. Damn, he looked good. I noticed my clothes were folded neatly on a chair. *Thoughtful.*

"I hope you're hungry. Here, come sit, and I'll bring you a plate." He motioned for me to take a seat at the dining table, where his workstation was set up on the other end. "Coffee?"

"Yes, please. Thank you," I said as I took a seat, eyeing his work area. "So, how's your writing coming along? Working on anything interesting?"

"I'm bouncing around a few ideas." He placed a fresh cup of coffee in front of me, complete with my pumpkin spice creamer, and then brushed his hand over my shoulder before going back to the kitchen.

Don't look at his ass. Don't look at his ass. I was totally looking at his ass. I mean, it was a fine ass, and we have established that we were, in fact, "fuck buddies" or whatever, so I could totally look at his ass, right? I raised my eyes to see Nathan looking directly at me. *Busted.* Again. His shit-eating grin was almost too adorable. He winked. My cheeks and chest flamed. This was at least the second time he had caught me ogling him. *Get it together, Daphne.* I licked my lips.

"Don't worry, Kitten, there's plenty of time for that later. Right now, you're gonna eat your breakfast like a good girl." Another wink from Nathan had me rolling my eyes at him and chuckling.

Nathan had made a delicious yet simple breakfast of bacon and eggs with toast. We made small talk throughout, and it wasn't nearly as awkward as I had expected. After breakfast, he said he was going to work a little more, so I took that opportunity to catch up on some reading. I was curled up on the couch in front of a roaring fire for most of the day while Nathan sat at the dining table, tapping away on his laptop.

It was comfortable, like we had been doing this for years. The sound of his typing was soothing, and even though we weren't engaging in conversation, it was nice to know he was there with me. I caught myself glancing up at him from time to time with a smile on my face. I know we said friends with benefits, but I knew it was just a matter of time before I fell head over heels for this man, and that scared the shit out of me.

It wasn't that I was opposed to falling in love again. My problem was that I didn't trust my judgment. Marcus had seemed great too when we first got together, so charismatic and attentive. He made me feel special every day until he didn't, and then he made me feel as if everything wrong in our relationship was my fault. By the end, I was conditioned to appease him and smooth things over when he was upset. I was thankful that I was able to see him for what he was and get out of that relationship, but how could I be sure that Nathan was any different? Sure, he appeared to be the perfect guy, but so had Marcus in the beginning.

I felt eyes on me, and when I looked up at Nathan, he smiled at me. I smiled back, knowing I was totally fucked.

17

NATHAN

Those eyes. I could get lost in her eyes forever. And that smile. I swear, every time she smiled at me, I felt it in my soul. Did I ever feel this way about Courtney? I don't think so, which is crazy, considering I was going to marry her. Sure, I loved her, or I thought I did, but there's no way I felt this strong of a pull to her. Things with Courtney had started great, of course. Don't they always? But as things progressed, I think she was more in love with the idea of being with me and my "fame" than she was actually in love with me. Toward the end, it felt as if we were going through the motions, but I thought it was just a rough patch we would get through after the stress of the wedding had died down.

Things have a way of working themselves out though, and Courtney sealed our fate when she had a tryst with some B-list celebrity. I was still hurt at the way it had gone down, but I wasn't sad about losing Courtney anymore, and I think that was mostly thanks to Daphne. She was a bright light in my world, and I was so very grateful that she stumbled into my life when she did. Was she ready to explore a relationship with me? Probably not, but I wouldn't give up. I knew we had met for a reason, and I was determined to see where this could go, even if that meant pretending my feelings for her didn't exist. For now.

We glanced at each other for only a moment before her eyes were drawn back to her book, but in that moment, I thought I felt a shift in her. Was she softening to the idea of us? I guess time would tell, but until then, I needed to keep my cool. She almost left this morning, and I couldn't stand the idea of it.

The day passed in quiet comfort. It was nice having her sitting in the same room as me while I worked. My fingers flew across my keyboard, laying down the plot of what I had hoped would be our story and our happily ever after. At least through my writing, I knew we'd find our happily ever after.

From her spot on the couch, I heard Daphne yawn and looked up to see her stretching with a sigh. She rose from the sofa and started for the kitchen. "Hungry?" she asked as she reached the refrigerator.

"Yeah, I could eat," I said with a wink and a grin.

That earned me a raised eyebrow. "Behave, I mean actual food," Daphne shot back while rummaging through our provisions.

"It's kind of late for lunch. How about an early dinner? I can order a pizza from that place in town, or we can go out?" I suggested.

Daphne shrugged. "No offense, but I think we should stay in or at least not be seen in town anymore together." She laughed. "You may be used to living in the spotlight, but I am definitely not."

"That's fair, so takeout then? I can go pick it up and I'll grab a few more things from the store to get us through the next couple of days," I offered.

"Okay, that sounds good. What are you in the mood for?" Daphne asked.

"You," I said with a wink. I was only half joking, "but I saw some menus in the drawer by the fridge. Why don't you see what our options are while I get changed?" She shook her head but then went to dig through the drawer with the menus while I made my way to my room.

When I returned to the kitchen, Daphne was bent over the island, facing away from me with her chin resting on her hands as she scanned the menus spread out before her. *I wish she were spread out before me,* I thought. I walked up behind her and placed a hand on the small of her back because, of course, I couldn't help myself, making her jump.

"Shit, oh my God, you scared the shit out of me," she said breathlessly, clutching her chest.

"Sorry, I didn't mean to. I swear." I motioned, crossing my heart, and vowed to remember this for the future. She was cute when she was spooked and breathless. "Find anything good?"

"Yeah, pizza is fine with me. When you mentioned it before, it sounded good, but I wanted to see what my options were. If I'm being honest, I could eat pizza every day. It's actually one of my favorite foods," she mentioned as she walked over to her bag that was slung across a dining table chair. She pulled out her wallet and started looking through it. "Here, let me get the pizza."

"Nope, I got it," I countered as I pulled on my jacket to leave.

"Listen, Nathan. You got lunch yesterday and groceries, and I still owe you for letting me crash in your rental. You've got to let me contribute somehow," she said as she tried to shove a fistful of money at me.

"Fine," I acquiesced, taking her money. "What toppings do you want? But I swear if you say any fruits, you're getting your own pizza."

Daphne pretended to be insulted and put a hand to her chest. "Excuse me, sir, but do I strike you as some sort of pizza heretic?" We laughed, and then she went on, "I'm pretty easygoing when it comes to pizza. No mushrooms or fruit, and I'll be good. But if you don't bring me crushed red peppers, you'll be dead to me."

"The only wrong answer there was pineapple, Daphne. I'm relieved to know you aren't a total psycho," I joked and walked toward the door. "Wait," I stopped and walked back to her, "let me put my number in your phone and then you can text me a list of what you need from the store while I'm out." Was this my sneaky way of getting her digits? Perhaps, but clearly, I wasn't above playing dirty. Surprisingly, she handed her phone to me, and I entered my number and then sent myself a text, so I had her number too. I handed her phone back. "Okay, I'll be back. Text me a list." She smiled, nodded her agreement, and gave a small wave as I was closing the front door.

18

DAPHNE

The door closed, and I turned to assess our food situation. If he was already going to the store, I might as well have him stock the place with some snacks and stuff to make meals for the next few days. I was going to be here for another four days, but then I had to return to reality. Ugh, reality, what would that look like when I got out of here?

Marcus kept texting and calling despite the fact that I hadn't responded to him. Thankfully, I had gotten all of my stuff out of his place before I came here, so that was one less thing to worry about when I got home. Where I was going to stay was another issue, though. Lexi's place was small, and while I knew I was more than welcome to crash there, it wasn't a permanent solution. After this fun escape from reality, I'd have to look for a place of my own.

That was a later problem, though. Now, I had to figure

out what we needed from the store. I went through the kitchen, noting what we had on hand, what we could make and what would get us through the next few days. When I was satisfied with my shopping list, I opened my phone to send Nathan a text. *Sex God.* I shook my head and laughed to myself. Of course, he couldn't put his actual name in my phone. Rolling my eyes, I typed out a message.

ME

Sex God, huh?

NATHAN

I mean, you're always screaming for God when I fuck you, so I figured it was fitting, Kitten.

ME

I'm changing your name to "full of himself." Anyway, here's the list of things we could use from the store. Thanks again for going into town.

NATHAN

Change my name to anything you want, but when I get home, you'll be screaming it.

Sweet Cheesus, the mouth on this man. *When he gets home.* Why did that sound so fucking good? And I was already wet thinking of the things he might do to me when he got here. I headed to my room to take a quick shower, shave all of my bits, and change into something a little less comfortable. But before I got in the shower, though, I shot off one last text.

ME

Prove it.

19

NATHAN

I stared at Daphne's last text while waiting for our pizza. I grinned to myself, the things I wanted to do to her. Thoughts of her spread out before me on the kitchen island this morning flashed through my mind, and I had to remind myself I was in public. I needed to think of literally anything else. The last thing I wanted to do was get caught with a hard-on in the pizza shop. Yet there I was, imagining all the things I'd do to her as soon as I got back to the cabin. Her last text made it abundantly clear that she was game. I liked this version of Daphne just as much, if not more, than the more cautious version she'd shown so far.

I had already grabbed the items from Daphne's list, but I still had to wait for the damn pizza—which was the last thing I wanted to eat when I got back. After what seemed like an eternity of waiting, I made my way out of town and back to the cabin in record time.

When I arrived back at the cabin, I made quick work of

unloading the car and getting everything inside. Daphne wasn't in the main area, and her door was closed. Perfect. I quickly disappeared into my room to freshen up and get a little more comfortable, a.k.a. a pair of gray sweatpants I knew were her weakness. I stopped by the full-length mirror in my room to admire my physique. I wouldn't say I was a vain man by any means, but I knew how I looked and I knew how others responded to my body. It had been hard-earned in the gym and with my daily runs, and I wasn't opposed to using it to help me seduce Daphne again. I dropped to the floor and got a few push-ups in, making my muscles bulge before I stepped out into the living room.

Walking into the main living area, I glimpsed Daphne walking out of her room and stopped dead in my tracks. She was stunning as usual, but what she was wearing had my jaw practically on the floor. She was in a short silk robe that was tied at the waist and hugged all of her curves. It was open slightly in the front, showcasing her ample breasts. Her hair fell in soft waves over her shoulders, and it looked like she had on a bit of makeup. My cock jumped to attention. Clearly, we were on the same page and I couldn't wait to see what was waiting for me under that robe.

She stopped when she saw me too and we stared at each other for a moment before she smiled, tucked a strand of hair behind her ear, and continued to me.

"I guess we had the same idea," she laughed as she crossed the room. "And here I thought I'd have to seduce you."

"No way, Baby. You told me to prove it, so I came ready

to do just that." I prowled toward her. "Damn, you look so good," I growled as I reached her. With one hand wrapped around her throat and the other around her waist, I leaned in to smell her neck. "Mmm, Baby, you smell good too." I licked up her neck and nipped at her ear. Her breath hitched as she leaned into my touch. Her hands were gripping my biceps and pulling me closer still. When her body was flush to mine, I whispered in her ear, "What did you change my name to in your phone, Kitten?"

"I didn't change it," she breathed.

"Good girl," I said as I removed my hand from her throat to untie her robe. I took a slight step away from her so I could see what was underneath. As the robe fell open, I was greeted by the sight of her sexy-as-hell lingerie made up of strappy black scraps of fabric. It covered her enough so that I couldn't see her nipples or her pussy, but that was about it. That image would be seared into my memory for as long as I lived. "Beautiful," the words fell from my mouth on an exhale. I moved my hand back up her body, brushing over her breast and grazing her nipple on my way back to her neck.

Her breathing became more labored as she ran her hands up my arms, down my chest, and then toyed with the waistband of my pants. She licked her lips and looked up at me through thick lashes. I couldn't wait another second and crashed my lips onto hers. We were a fury of lips, tongues, and teeth. As much as I wanted to take my time and savor every inch of her, I was overcome with need.

Apparently, so was she because, without warning, she

dropped to her knees and pulled my pants down with her. As I stepped out of my pants, she shrugged off her robe, and I could appreciate her lingerie fully. There was a tie at her breast and two more on her hips. It was like Christmas morning, and she was my gift waiting to be unwrapped. I had barely a moment to take her in before her nails were scraping down my thighs, bringing my attention fully back to her at my feet.

"Now I think I remember something about making you scream my name, Kitten, but right now, I want to hear you gagging on my cock." My dick was painfully hard and begging for her to ease my suffering. With another lick of her lips, she leaned forward and took me to the back of her throat and then swallowed. She gagged, and I swear I almost came right then and there. I would never tire of her on her knees before me with my cock in her mouth. "Baby, I'm going to fuck your throat now, okay? If it's too much, give me a couple of taps on my thigh."

She looked up at me as she popped my dick out of her mouth. "Do your worst, Sex God." She rolled her eyes at me.

What a brat.

"Such a brat, Daphne," I said as I grabbed the back of her head with both hands and pushed into her again. "Let's see if that smart mouth can take all of me." She gagged on me and then looked me right in the eyes as she… Was she smiling at me from around my cock? This fucking woman. I thrust a little deeper and more force-fully. I was careful not to go too hard or deep yet, as I didn't want to hurt her, but I was going to push her limits a bit tonight.

I usually preferred to be more dominant in the bedroom, but when I showed that side of myself depended on the woman I was with. Tonight was the night I wanted to show Daphne all of me. While I had a feeling she'd be into it, there was always a chance she wouldn't. It was a chance I was willing to take because I had it bad for this woman, and if we had even a chance at something, I wanted her to know what she was getting herself into.

Another gag brought me back to the moment. I grasped her chin and angled her the way I wanted as I drove in again, harder this time. She hummed around my cock, and I swear I could feel it all the way in my toes. I couldn't take my eyes off her as I kept fucking her throat. I wasn't all the way in, but every time I got to the back of her throat, she tried to swallow me down even further. Her hands had been gripping my thighs, and as I watched her right hand fall between her legs, I almost fucking came. She pushed the scrap of fabric that was covering her pussy to the side and started playing with her clit. Holy shit. "Fuck yes, Baby. That's so fucking hot." She continued to rub herself in tight circles while moaning around my girth. That was it—I couldn't wait any longer. I had planned on doling out her punishment for much longer, but this girl was sucking the life out of me, and her playing with herself while she did it had me on the brink. "I want you to make yourself come, Kitten. I'm not gonna last."

There we were in the middle of the living room, her on

her knees fucking herself with her fingers while I fucked her mouth. She was calling out around my cock, and I knew she was close, so I tightened my grip on her throat. Her eyes grew wide, her movements became unsteady, and as I thrust in again even deeper, she came, soaking my feet and the floor.

At the sight, I came with a roar, and she drank down every drop. "Such a good girl, taking all of me," I praised her as I stroked her cheek. Her mascara was running down her face, and she'd never looked more beautiful as she smiled up at me. I wasted no time scooping her up in my arms. I kicked my sweatpants over the mess we had made on the floor and marched us into my bedroom.

20

DAPHNE

I was dazed as Nathan placed me down on his bed. I can't remember ever making myself come like that before. Was it because Nathan's cock was choking me or because of his filthy mouth, or a combination of the two? Whatever the reason, I wanted to do it again and again. I liked that Nathan had taken charge, and I didn't have to think about what was happening. Speaking of which… Nathan parted my legs and made his way between my thighs. His mouth was so close to my sensitive clit and I tried to angle my hips so that he would touch me.

"Patience, Kitten," he breathed against my sex. "Your pussy is so greedy, you want more already?"

"Yes," I panted while thrusting my hips into him.

He chuckled as he swiped his tongue through my already dripping folds. "Baby, you were being a brat earlier and I think it's time to teach you a lesson." He sat up, grabbed my ankles, and flipped me onto my stomach. He leaned over me, pressed his body against mine, and whispered in my ear, "Daphne, this is serious. Are you okay with me spanking you?"

I started to panic, "Wh…what? You want to hit me?" I had never been hit by a man before, not in an aggressive way and not in a sexual way either. I honestly wasn't sure if I would love it or hate it.

"It's a punishment of sorts, but I promise to make you feel good. If you don't like it, you tell me to stop any time," he explained.

"Um, okay, I guess." My face flamed. I was just on my knees, choking his cock down, but letting him spank me made me feel embarrassed for some reason. "Do we need a safe word or something?" I asked nervously.

What the fuck was I getting myself into?

"No need for safe words, Baby. You say stop, and I stop. It's that simple. Do you trust me?" Nathan was still pressed up against me and I could feel his thick, hard shaft pressing between my ass cheeks. Did I trust this man? Oddly enough, I did, and I wanted to have this new experience with him despite my embarrassment. When was the next time a man was going to want to try this? Maybe I needed to try it once while in this situationship to see if it was something I liked.

"Yes. I don't know why, but I do trust you, Nathan," I breathed.

"Good girl," he growled as he licked my neck and then he moved off me, but I barely had time to mourn the loss of him as he grabbed my ankles and pulled me toward the edge of the bed. His hands caressed my thighs and over the curve of my ass. "Now get on your knees."

I did as I was told, and he continued to smooth his hands over my body. It felt amazing and electrifying, but the anticipation was killing me. I wanted more, so I leaned into his touch.

"Tsk tsk," he chided as he continued his all too gentle assault. "Patience, Daphne." He stroked over my ass and grazed my folds, but not nearly how I wanted him to. I was writhing around, trying to get some much-needed friction to no avail. Nathan placed one hand on the small of my back. "Stay still, Kitten."

I froze. My breathing was heavy and uneven. I was so turned on, and he wasn't even doing anything. How? And then, without warning, he thrust two fingers inside my dripping pussy. I cried out, not because it hurt, but because I was surprised and it felt so good to be filled by him. He pumped those fingers in and out of me a few times, and then his thumb found my clit, making me jump. He toyed with me like that until he brought me right to the edge of orgasm, only for him to withdraw his fingers and leave me gasping.

"Nathan, please," I begged, thrusting my hips back to him.

Smack. I gasped. My pussy clenched around nothing. My right ass cheek flamed, and then I felt him smooth over the spot with his hand. Another smack and then again, he smoothed over the spot to soothe it. He repeated this pattern a few more times, and each time, my pussy clenched, begging to be filled. "You doing okay, Baby?" Nathan asked.

"Mmm hmm," I cooed, leaning into his touch.

"Oh, you like this, don't you?" Nathan continued to rub his hands over my ass and thighs.

When his hand moved to the apex of my thighs and grazed my clit, I moaned, "More."

"Move up on the bed." Nathan directed me further onto the bed. "Put your hands here." He motioned to the headboard.

I did as instructed and braced for the next strike, but nothing came. I turned to look behind me to see him sitting back on his heels, stroking himself. "Uh-uh, Kitten. Face the headboard." I reluctantly turned back around. I was so turned on, I thought I'd explode. I tried to calm my breathing and be patient, though all I wanted to do was say fuck it and turn around and jump this man.

The bed dipped behind me as Nathan edged closer, and then I felt him at my entrance. He rubbed the head of his dick through my folds and over my clit. I ground back into him, wanting more. He continued rubbing over my sensitive nub over and over until I was back on the brink of an orgasm, only to stop just before.

Another smack came down hard on my ass as he thrust his cock inside of me. I came so fucking hard I saw stars, and my body started to convulse. "Good girl. Come on Daddy's dick." Nathan roared behind me as he continued to fuck me from behind, occasionally giving my ass a firm slap. My hands eventually slipped from the headboard, and I clawed the bedsheets, screaming into a pillow as I came again.

At some point, Nathan must have come too, but I don't recall when or how it happened. Had I passed out? I don't know, but the next thing I knew, I was being lowered into the warm, bubbly water in Nathan's tub. He whispered more words of praise as he washed every inch of me. I vaguely recall being lifted out of the tub, dried off, and then being carried to my room. Nathan tucked me in and kissed me on the forehead before leaving me there as I drifted off to sleep.

I had never been fucked like that. Ever. In my day-to-day life, I was always in charge, caring for patients, making critical decisions, and being responsible for others. It felt so good to let go and let Nathan take control and then take care of me afterward. We had only known each other for a few days, but I knew I could trust him to take care of me. I never trusted Marcus like this, and I think that was very telling.

The next day, I woke up earlier than usual and started the coffee. Nathan wasn't up yet, which was odd. He was usually up and had the coffee made before I could even think about getting out of bed. I was enjoying my time off from the hospital and taking my rest very seriously, so sleeping in had been a priority this week.

Since my arrival, I really hadn't had a chance to take a look around outside except for gazing through the large windows that overlooked the lake, so I headed out for a walk and explored the area surrounding the cabin. After pulling on a pair of fleece leggings, a thick hoodie, and my boots, I made my way out to the living room.

The cabin itself was a dream. The side that faced the water was a peaked wall made entirely of windows. As I stepped out onto the deck, a cool autumn breeze greeted me. It wasn't cold enough for a heavier jacket today, but the bite in the air was refreshing. Situated almost right on the edge of the water, the steps from the deck led right onto the rocky beach. There was a small fire pit area steps away, surrounded by several Adirondack chairs. Just slightly further down the beach was a wooden dock that extended out onto the lake.

I walked down the beach to the dock, taking in my surroundings. It was so peaceful here. I wondered what this place was like in the winter, with snow on the trees and ice on the lake. Did it ice over? Could you ice skate on it? I imagined myself swimming here in the summer. Although I wanted to come back and check it out during different seasons, fall had always been my favorite. I couldn't imagine a more perfect time to be here.

Leaves crunched under my feet as I made my way down the beach by the edge of the forest. The wind picked up, and I pulled up my hood and thrust my hands into the pocket of my hoodie. Maybe I should have grabbed a jacket. My mind wandered back to the morning and my last couple of days here with Nathan. He was unlike any man I had met before. Funny, caring, could eat pussy and fuck like a god, yet he wasn't full of himself at all. I was dangerously close to falling for this man, and I knew staying here for even one more day was a mistake. Unfortunately for my heart, it was a mistake I was willing to make.

After walking for far longer than I had intended, I made my way back to the cabin. My nose was chilled, and I had started shivering. *Yep, definitely should have worn a jacket and maybe a hat and gloves. Oops.* As the cabin came back into sight, I was thankful to see smoke billowing from the chimney. I couldn't wait to warm up in front of the fire and then take a scalding hot shower.

As I got closer, I heard loud voices coming from the cabin, so I picked up my pace. All I could think was that Marcus had somehow found me, and that he and Nathan had gotten into it. But how? I had immediately stopped sharing my location with him when I left our apartment. I didn't know how he had found me. All I knew was that I was afraid for Nathan because I wasn't sure of what Marcus was truly capable of. I was in a panic as I rushed up the steps and onto the porch.

I burst through the door and then froze in my tracks.

21

NATHAN

I woke up later than usual, feeling well-rested and excited for the day. Even though today would have been Courtney's and my wedding day, I wasn't feeling sad or upset. In fact, I was feeling hopeful for the future. A future that I desperately wanted to include Daphne. But would she want that? I knew that our friends-with-benefits situation had an expiration date, but I wanted more.

I stretched in bed, recalling our night together. She was so responsive to me. Her pussy clenched around me every time I smacked her luscious ass. I stroked my cock at the thought. Another stroke, and I was debating going to her and burying myself in her again, but a banging on the front door brought me back into the present. Who could that be? Did Daphne go out and forget the code?

Smiling to myself, I got up and threw on my lowest-hanging gray sweatpants but skipped the shirt. If it was

Daphne, maybe I could entice her for another round, and if it wasn't her, well, I guess whoever it was was in for a treat.

My smile immediately fell when I opened the door and came face-to-face with Courtney. She smiled slyly as her eyes raked down my body. "Hey babe," she said sweetly as if she hadn't cheated on me and we didn't break up, and slipped past me in the doorway. I must have been too stunned to stop her because I barely registered she had made it into the cabin.

I closed the door and turned to face her. Courtney was dressed in a low-cut, skin-tight sweater dress with her tits on full display. As if that was helping her case. It wasn't. I knew beyond a shadow of a doubt that I was completely over her. Nothing she could say or do would change that. "What are you doing here, Courtney? And how did you even find me?"

"I missed you so much, babe, and I thought we should talk. We were supposed to be getting married today," Courtney whined.

"There's nothing to talk about. You cheated; we're done. I've moved on." I walked past her into the kitchen to start the coffee I was definitely going to need today, only to find it already brewed. I glanced over to Daphne's room. Her door was closed, but knowing she had already made coffee made me nervous about her whereabouts. Hopefully, I could get rid of Courtney before she emerged. I had nothing to hide from her, but I also didn't want her to have to deal with Courtney's crazy ass.

"Moved on? You mean with that mousy-looking bitch

you were photographed with? Are you with *her*?" She sneered, looking disgusted. Mousy? Daphne? No freaking way. Daphne was a total smoke show with her curvy figure and full, pouty lips. Every inch of her was sexy as hell, and the last word I'd use to describe her would be mousy.

"First of all, she's not a bitch, Courtney. Second, it's none of your business if I am. You lost any right to know about my life when you slept with someone else. *You* cheated on *me*, remember?" I was losing my patience, and my voice was getting louder. "You need to leave, now." I moved toward her. She had to go, even if I had to physically remove her from the cabin.

As I got closer, she threw herself at me, wrapping her arms around my neck and clinging to me like her life depended on it. "I need you, Nate. I made a mistake," she sobbed into my chest. "I love you." Oh God, was she crying? I rolled my eyes up to the ceiling and took a deep breath, keeping my arms straight down at my sides. She's the one who cheated. Cheating was a deal breaker for me, and there was no coming back from that.

"I told you, you can't be here, Courtney." I raised my voice more, "We aren't together anymore." I tried to extricate myself from her embrace as she continued to cling to me. It was at that moment that the door to the back porch opened and Daphne walked in. Well, fuck me. This looked bad. I quickly grabbed Courtney by her wrists and placed them at her sides. Courtney continued to struggle against me and then turned her attention to Daphne.

"Oh my God, Nathan, what the fuck is she doing here?"

Courtney screeched as she stepped away from me. Daphne was still standing in the doorway, staring at us.

"Courtney, it's none of your business what she's doing here. Now, get the fuck out," I shouted as I attempted to usher her to the front door. Daphne headed to the kitchen, and it looked like she had gotten the bourbon out. Good, I was gonna need that. Wait, what time is it? Didn't matter.

"I'm pregnant!" Courtney screamed when I had her almost to the door.

"Liar. You have an IUD, remember?" I reminded her. "And even if you were, it wouldn't be mine."

She started sobbing again. "Well, I could be, ya know? It's not 100% effective."

"Get out," I said once again as I opened the front door and deposited her on the porch. I followed her out and closed the door. "Look, Courtney, we're done. You knew cheating was a deal breaker for me, and you fucked that guy anyway. You made your choice, and us not being together is the consequence of that choice. Be gone when I get back. I mean it. There's nothing left between us."

I turned and walked back into the cabin and closed the door behind me. I leaned back into it, closed my eyes, and exhaled a breath. After a moment, I walked into the kitchen, where Daphne met me, holding out a glass of bourbon. "Drink?" she offered.

"Yeah, sorry about that. I must have forgotten to turn off my location sharing, but I never expected her to just show up," I said as I gratefully took the bourbon from her.

"I thought you could use a drink. That seemed intense," Daphne said with a chuckle.

"I mean, I usually don't drink this early, but I feel like this is an acceptable reason to make an exception," I laughed. "Sorry. You didn't need to see that."

"It's no problem, and it isn't your fault. It was pretty clear you didn't want her here, but also, it wasn't my place to get involved, so I figured I'd let you handle it," Daphne said as she sipped her glass of bourbon. "Wanna talk about it?"

"Not particularly," I admitted. "It's been over since before she cheated, but that was the nail in the coffin for us. She didn't believe me when I told her it was over the first time, I guess. Today was supposed to be our wedding day, and it looks like she had some feelings about that." After another swig of my drink, I continued, "Honestly, I was afraid you were going to be mad she was here. I thought maybe you'd try to leave again."

"Oh no, you don't have to worry about me getting jealous. I'm not the type, especially since you made it clear we're just friends with benefits or whatever. I don't have any claim on you." *Ouch.* Daphne shrugged. "Anyway, it didn't seem like you wanted her here, so it's kind of a moot point. But seriously, are you okay? With today supposed to be your wedding day, how are you feeling?"

"Yeah, I'm okay, and you actually have a lot to do with that. I've enjoyed having you here, and I'm glad you didn't bail on me. I think I'm gonna need a drinking buddy today."

I grinned. This was exactly what I needed today—a fun day with my new favorite person.

22

DAPHNE

What the fuck? When I walked into the cabin and saw Nathan up close and personal with that gorgeous blonde, I was fighting my internal rage demon so hard. It took everything in me to stay cool and not freak the fuck out. But why was I so upset? I'll tell you why… because clearly, I have feelings for this man that I didn't expect to have. I had no business being jealous. We weren't together. He made it perfectly clear that he didn't want anything serious with me. This was just sex, and I thought I was okay with that.

Was I okay with that?

I thought I was, but when I walked in and saw them together, my chest hurt. I was so disappointed when I thought for that initial moment that they were in an intimate embrace. Sure, he was charismatic and handsome and funny, but neither of us was in a position to start a new relationship. Courtney obviously wasn't done with him, though it seemed like he was done with her. I definitely couldn't risk more with him, especially now. What if he changed his mind? What if she kept coming back, and they decided to work things out? That's why I couldn't get involved more than I already was. I had to protect my heart, and I had no business acting like a jealous girlfriend. I wasn't his girlfriend—I was a fun post-engagement hookup to him, right?

Whatever it was between us, I had to keep my shit together. The last thing he needed was another stage five clinger like his ex. I would have to play the cool girl even though inside, I was freaking out. I took another sip of my bourbon and winced. Why was I drinking bourbon at 8:00 a.m.? I hadn't even had my coffee yet. Welp, I guess that's how this day was going to go.

"You okay?" Nathan asked, pulling me out of my thoughts.

"Yeah, sorry. I'm good." I raised my glass in his direction. "Cheers?" I shrugged and gave him a lopsided grin.

"Ha, yeah, cheers." He laughed, "I guess day drinking is in order." Nathan took a long pull from his glass and leaned against the island. "So, what did you have planned today?"

"Me? Oh, you know, the usual. Scrolling social media, reading, and apparently drinking is now on the agenda." My eyes widened as I took another sip.

"I thought maybe we'd go into town today, but I think that's off the table in case Courtney is still lingering around. You okay with staying in? We could watch movies or play board games? Order delivery later?" He looked so excited by the mere thought of staying in and hanging out, playing games.

Gah, why was he so damn cute?

"Sounds good to me, but I think we need actual food first, or this is going to be a very short day for me. I'm a lightweight." I went to the fridge to gather supplies. "How do you feel about pancakes?"

"Love them, actually." Nathan sat at the island while I got to work on breakfast and coffee because even if we were day drinking, I needed caffeine.

"So today was supposed to be the wedding," I started. "If you don't want to talk about it, I totally understand, but how are you okay? I'd think it would be a hard day for you."

"I honestly thought it would be too when I first got here, but looking back at our relationship and the breakup, I think things were over before she cheated. The wedding planning masked a lot of our issues, and when she cheated, it was the last straw for me. And it may sound corny, but I think your being here has a lot to do with my being okay today. I've really enjoyed spending this time with you, and not just because the sex is out of this world." He winked.

My cheeks flamed. Sex with Nathan *was* out of this world, but he was right; that wasn't all. We had connected on a deeper level, and we've had nothing but fun and easy conversations since we met. "Yeah, the sex is pretty good, but I know what you mean."

Nathan raised an eyebrow. "Pretty good, huh? I'll remember that." He winked again and then looked at his phone, which was vibrating on the island. "I gotta take this. Be right back," he said and then stood and strode into his room.

I continued making breakfast—pancakes with fresh fruit and bacon on the side. It looked and smelled so good, but Nathan wasn't back yet, and I didn't want to start without him. I went to his room, where his door was cracked open. "I promise I'm okay, Dad. You don't have to worry about me." I heard Nathan say from the other side of the door. "Listen, I gotta go, but I promise I'll stop by after my trip and we'll catch up."

I realized he was finishing up his call, so I quickly made my way back to the kitchen and waited for him to reemerge. He came walking back moments later. "It smells so good, Daphne. Thanks for making breakfast."

"No problem. It's ready if you want to go sit at the table." I gathered up our plates and brought them to the dining table, where I had already set our coffees and condiments.

"Everything okay?" I asked, nodding toward his phone that was still in his hand.

"Oh yeah," he said, putting his phone face down on the table. "It was my dad checking in to make sure I was okay today."

"Are you close to your dad?" I asked as I dug into my pancakes.

"Yeah, I am. We've always been close, but we got closer when my mom got sick. I was there a lot to help out while my brothers handled things at the shop. My dad took a big step back from the business when Mom got sick. She was the love of his life, and losing her tore him apart. He stopped going into the shop, and my brothers stepped in to take over the day-to-day stuff right after she died. And since he's not been occupied with work, my brothers and I try to spend as much time with him as possible."

"My God, I can't imagine going through that, either as a child or as a partner. That must have been so hard on all of you, but I'm glad he has you and your brothers." Shit, I was trying to be the fun girl and keep things light today, but this conversation was getting heavy. Both of my parents were alive and well, still as in love as the day they got married. I couldn't imagine losing either of them or what it would be like to lose the love of my life if I ever found him. I must have been staring off into space, deep in thought, because when Nathan cleared his throat, I jumped. "Shit, sorry, I was a little lost in thought there."

"It's okay. Sorry things got heavy there."

"No, it's totally okay. I asked because I wanted to know more about you and your family. It seems like you all have pretty great relationships. But I am so sorry about your mom." I gave him a small smile and reached my hand out to cover his.

He smiled back at me. "Thank you. That really means a lot. Seriously, I'm glad you're here, Daphne."

The rest of breakfast passed in quiet comfort. We talked more about his family and made small talk. After we finished breakfast and our first glass of bourbon, I decided to shower and have another cup of coffee to wake up, so I retreated to my room.

When I came back out of my room, Nathan had moved into the living room and had blankets and pillows spread out in front of the fire. On the blankets, he had set up a board game, and as I got closer, I started laughing.

"Operation? You're not serious!" Of all the games to find in this cabin, he chose Operation.

"You're a nurse, right? This is right up your alley," he laughed.

"First of all, I'm not *that* kind of nurse. And second, technically surgeons perform the actual operations." I rolled my eyes and pretended to be annoyed.

"Tomato, tomaatto," he exaggerated with a wink. Damn this man and his ability to make me laugh. I made myself comfortable on the blankets and propped myself up on some pillows. Nathan handed me a glass. Okay, I guess he was serious about day drinking. We clinked them together. "Cheers! And may the best *man* win," he said smugly.

"We'll see about that," I said as I grabbed the tweezers to start my turn. Bzzzzzzz. Fuck.

"Drink." Nathan motioned to the glass I had set down.

"Oh, no fucking way. I agreed to drink with you. I didn't agree to make this into a drinking game. I'll freaking die," I huffed.

"Come on, Daphne, live a little," Nathan coaxed.

"Fine, but I'm telling you now, you won't like me when I'm praying to the porcelain god and you have to hold my hair back." I tipped back my glass and took a small sip.

"Come to think of it, I don't think I'll like you much either, then."

Nathan laughed, and it was a laugh that seemed to come from his very soul. It was a laugh I very much wanted to hear more often. Okay, so maybe this was a good idea. I made it my mission to keep winning and keep my sips small. This was going to be fun.

23

NATHAN

Daphne was shitfaced. We'd been playing games for a few hours. We started with Operation, which, oddly enough, she was absolutely terrible at, and moved on to what I thought was going to be a better game for her. Turns out Monopoly was not her game either. Neither was War, unfortunately for her. She talked so much shit through it all, even though she was losing and drinking way more than me. I almost felt bad for her, but then she'd talk more shit and that feeling would just float away.

Daphne was laughing at, I wasn't sure what, while rolling over the pillows that were spread out on the floor. She was adorable, but she was definitely going to be hurting later, so I decided it was time to feed her and probably get her to bed. "How do you feel about Chinese food for dinner?" I asked her when her giggling died down.

She sat straight up and looked me in the eye with a seriousness I hadn't seen since breakfast. "Oh, hell yes! I love Chinese. I would kill for some lo mein right now."

"Okay, I'll order for delivery. Want anything else?" She had face-planted into a stack of pillows and was kicking her feet in the air. I guess I was making the decisions about food tonight.

I called and placed our order and then returned to the living room to stoke the fire, only to find Daphne was now passed out with her mouth hanging open, drooling on a pillow. The food was still a little way out, so I took a quick rinse before it arrived.

In the shower, I couldn't help the smile that stained my face. Daphne was so carefree and fun. We didn't stop laughing all day. I had almost totally forgotten that today would have been my wedding day, and that Courtney had shown up here this morning to cause a scene. I was grateful that Daphne was here, and that she was so understanding of my situation. Wait. Was it that she was understanding, though, or that she had totally friend-zoned me and didn't even care Courtney had shown up? Shit. It was my idea to be "friends with benefits," but that's not what I wanted at all. Did I shoot myself in the foot by suggesting it? My mind raced as I quickly finished my shower, dressed, and returned to the living room.

Daphne was right where I had left her, lightly snoring away. How was she so adorable, even snoring and drooling on the floor? Damn, I had it bad. I was staring at her like a moron when the doorbell jarred me out of my thoughts. The doorbell also woke Daphne, but I turned quickly, hopefully without her noticing me being a total creeper.

After I collected our food and brought it to the living room, I went to the kitchen to get us some much-needed nonalcoholic drinks and plates. I thought Daphne could use a break from the bourbon, and I'd had enough too. When I returned, Daphne was sitting up and looked a little more with it. "Hmmm, this smells amazing." She practically moaned as she started going through the bags.

I had gotten a little of everything because I was pretty hungry myself and unsure of what she'd like. "I figured we could share a little of everything if that's okay?" I asked as I passed her a plate.

"That's perfect." She smiled and dug in. "Oh my God, you got egg rolls? Fuck yeah!" I smiled back at her as she stuffed the whole egg roll in her mouth and chomped loudly. Well, I'm glad we'd passed that awkward stage. You know when the girl pretends to eat less or more politely to impress the guy? Or was this her not being interested in me? Did she feel comfortable, or was she drunk, or was she not trying to win me over? Fuck, I was going to go insane thinking about this. I couldn't wait until tomorrow. Tomorrow, I'd tell her how I felt. I knew it was crazy to have feelings like this for someone so soon, but I did, and I couldn't keep lying to myself or her anymore.

"Hey, quit eating all my egg rolls!" I teased and snatched them away from her.

She huffed at me and rolled her eyes. "Rude." And then

dug into the next dish. Dish after dish, we ate like two starved people until we couldn't possibly eat more.

"Sweet lord, I couldn't eat another bite if you paid me." Daphne sighed, "That was delicious. Who would've thought such a small town would have such good Chinese food?"

"Seriously, that was amazing, but now I just want to sleep. The booze and this fire aren't helping," I laughed.

"Why don't we watch a movie?" Daphne suggested. "Let's get cozy, and if we fall asleep, so be it."

"Sounds like a plan. I'll clean up. You pick a movie." I gathered up our leftovers and dirty dishes and took them to the kitchen. I returned with fresh water for both of us and the fortune cookies that had been at the bottom of the takeout bag. "We missed the fortune cookies," I said as I made my way back to the living room.

"Oh no, I couldn't eat another bite right now. Let's save them for later." She patted the space next to her for me to sit. "I picked a real scary one this time." She grinned.

"Oh great," I laughed in response. "Another movie you'll only half watch through your fingers because you're scared."

She slapped my arm and smiled. "Whatever. Lie down and get comfy. I wanna snuggle."

I guess the booze was still lowering her inhibitions because Daphne didn't usually want to snuggle. In fact, except for the times we'd had sex, she usually kept her distance. I didn't need to be asked twice, though, so I fluffed up some pillows, grabbed the softest of the blankets, and laid down next to her. She proceeded to lie down and placed her head in the crux where my arm met my body and melted into me with the softest sigh as I covered us both with the blanket.

Ten minutes later, Daphne was sound asleep, and I turned the movie off. I was completely content lying there with her in my arms, listening to the sound of her breathing and the crackling of the fire. I gently stroked her back and played with her hair, imagining what it would be like to do this every day. My mind was made up. Tomorrow, I was going to tell Daphne how I felt. I wanted to explore a relationship with her, and I hoped she'd want the same.

24

———————

DAPHNE

Ouch! My neck was killing me. Wiping the sleep from my eyes, I took in my surroundings. The room was barely lit by the fire that was almost out in the fireplace. There was drool trailing from my mouth and pooling on… what the fuck? There was a puddle of drool on Nathan's chest. His shirt was soaked. Fuck me. This was embarrassing on multiple levels. I quickly attempted to extricate myself from the situation, but as I was trying to get up, Nathan pulled me in closer against him.

"Where do you think you're going?" he groaned in the sexiest, sleepy voice I had ever heard.

"To bed. But I think, um, you might need a towel. Sorry." I motioned to the puddle on his shirt. I was mortified, but I owned up to the mess since there wasn't any other way to explain the drool fest away.

"Mmm," was his only response as he pulled me back

down and rolled me over and onto his other side, spooning me from behind. He nuzzled his face into my neck, inhaling deeply. Did he just smell me?

I tried to pry him off me. "Nathan, I need to pee," I whined, hoping he'd let me up.

"Good try, Kitten," he chuckled. "Now be a good girl and go back to sleep. I'm comfy."

Ugh. This felt too good. I had to get up and get away from him. I was still a little drunk, but not drunk enough to let myself stay in his embrace. I waited until his breathing evened out and I was sure that he was asleep before I attempted to get up again. I carefully slipped out of his grasp, covered him with a blanket, and quietly made my way to my room. I needed Lexi to talk some sense into me. She was, after all, the queen of having sex without feelings.

"Sup, whore?" she answered my call after the first ring.

"I need to be talked off the ledge. I think I'm falling for this man, and I know that's a terrible idea and terrible timing, but he's just so…perfect? I don't know. I think I might still be drunk. But he's so hot and nice and fun and did I mention he's smokin' hot?" I rambled on, barely taking a breath.

"Whoa. Take a breath. Why are you drunk? It's like 7:00 p.m.," Lexi chuckled.

"So today was supposed to be his wedding day and his ex showed up here."

"No fucking way! What happened? I need the deets." Lexi loved drama. Well, let me be clear, she loved other people's drama. When it came to her personal life, she avoided drama and attachments at all costs.

I laughed. "It was pretty drama-free. Courtney came, she begged Nathan to take her back, and he shot her down."

"Borrriinnnnggg!" I could practically hear Lexi's eyes rolling to the back of her head. "So what? She just left, and you guys just decided to drink all day? Please tell me you were at least naked all day too."

"Nope. Sorry to be such a disappointment. We drank, played board games, and ate Chinese food. It was a pretty fun day. Then I fell asleep on him on the living room floor and drooled all over his chest, which was a little embarrassing, but he didn't seem to mind." I smiled to myself as I recalled our day together.

"Okay, so what's the problem then? You don't want to fall for him, but you are? What's the issue? If you like him, why not explore that?" I looked down at my phone to make sure the call was still connected to the right person.

"I'm sorry, who is this? And what have you done with Lexi?" I joked.

"Har. Har. Har," she deadpanned. "Listen, you know I'm all for a good old 'fuck 'n' run' situation, but if you actually have feelings for this guy, then why not just see what happens? Maybe you aren't built for this fuck buddy shit."

She was right, of course. Lexi knew me better than anyone, and she knew I was a relationship girl. I was never promiscuous in college. I went from relationship to relationship, but wasn't that exactly why I shouldn't jump into yet another one?

"I may not be, but I also think it's too soon for both of us to be getting involved in something potentially serious. I've always gone from relationship to relationship, and maybe I need time to myself to heal and figure out what I want. Lexi, I don't even have a place to live. If I start something with Nathan, who's to say we won't move too quickly and move in together, and then I'm right back in another Marcus situation?"

"First of all, slow down. I think you're getting *way* too ahead of yourself. You're already talking about moving in with him? I just said maybe you should explore what's there, not marry the guy. Jeez. Second, if you think you need some alone time, then I support that decision. And as far as the place to stay, you know you can stay with me for as long as you need to." She was right. I had to calm down and get my priorities straight. Priority number one was me and my heart. I didn't need to complicate my life more than it already was by getting involved in yet another doomed-to-fail relationship.

"You're right, but I don't think now is the time to explore a new relationship. As much as I do like Nathan, I also know I'm not ready. Plus, his ex literally showed up here today. I don't know if he's ready for a new relationship either, since this whole 'friends with benefits' thing was his idea. If he wanted more, wouldn't he say something?"

"Listen, I'm team Daphne no matter what and I'll support whatever you decide to do, even if it involves getting rid of a body." She laughed on the other end of the call, but I knew she was deadly serious. I knew I could count on her for anything.

"Thank you, but I highly doubt I'd ever call you to help me get rid of a body." I chuckled back.

"You never know."

"Okay, well thanks, I guess." My tone was steeped in sarcasm. "I'm gonna take a bath and hopefully sleep off this alcohol. I'm definitely going to spend the rest of the night hiding in my room and avoiding that handsome man in the living room."

"Ugh, you're hopeless. If you're so sure you don't want a relationship, you can at least have some more fun before you come home," Lexi chided.

"I'm *hopeless*? You're hopeless, and when you eventually meet *the one*, I'm going to thoroughly enjoy saying I told you so," I laughed. "Love you. Talk to you soon."

"Love you too, hoe bag. Enjoy your bath." We ended the call, and I lay back on my bed with a sigh. My mind was all over the place. I was so back and forth about Nathan, but I knew that was the exact reason I couldn't let this go any further. I needed to take time for myself. After all, that was supposed to be the whole point of this trip.

I groaned as I forced myself out of bed and into the en suite to start my bath. I had found the most delightful-smelling lavender bubble bath in the bathroom the day before and decided to give it a try. I ran my hand under the warm water as the scent of lavender filled the room, and I daydreamed about what a life with Nathan could be. I was lost in thought when there was a knock at the bedroom door.

"Hey, are you okay?" Nathan asked through the closed door.

"Fine. Just going to take a bath and sleep it off," I called back over the sound of the tub filling.

"You want some company?" Nathan asked with too much hope in his voice. But was it hope at the prospect of another night of sex, or was it the hope of more? I was so in my head I couldn't possibly imagine what was going on in his.

"I'm good. I think I'm going to relax and then get to bed early. I'll see you in the morning, Nathan." I did my best to keep my voice friendly and cool, though my insides were screaming at me to let him in to defile me yet again.

"You sure you're okay?" He sounded worried, so I went to the door to put him at ease.

I opened the door a crack and smiled up at him. "I'm fine. I promise. I need to sleep this off. Alone." I gave him another smile as I started to shut the door.

Nathan put his hand up to stop the door. "Okay, but if you need a hand, I'd be happy to wash your back." He winked and then retreated with a grin. The door clicked closed, and the image of him behind me in the bath, caressing my curves, filled my head. Just the thought of him touching me in any capacity had me so needy for him. My body thrummed, and my pulse quickened. This man made me absolutely feral for him. I shook my head and headed back to the tub, which was now full.

I removed my clothes and sunk into the warm water, submerging myself completely. I stayed under for a few moments, trying to clear my mind, but when I surfaced, he was still at the forefront of my thoughts. I came here to have some time to myself and clear my head, and all I've done is fuck myself up even more. Nathan was consuming my every thought, and I had to get the hell out of here.

25

NATHAN

Walking away from Daphne's room had me feeling uneasy. Maybe it was the alcohol, and she needed to sleep it off, but I had the nagging feeling that something else was going on. We had only known each other for four days, so it was absolutely bat shit crazy that I could have genuine feelings for her, right? But my feelings for her felt real enough, and I knew I had to tell her. I wanted to date her and see where this could go, but I think I fucked up trying to do the whole friends-with-benefits thing.

I decided I could use some advice. Even though my brothers were clueless when it came to relationships, they were better than nothing.

ME

Mayday, mayday.

DYLAN

Oh shit, what happened now?

BRANDON

👀

ME

Soooo yesterday Daphne almost left, and I convinced her to stay under the guise of being fuck buddies.

DYLAN

BRANDON

😐

ME

Listen, I was desperate to keep her around until I could convince her to give me a real shot. I know it was probably a mistake, but it kept her around and we have been having a lot of fun. And then Courtney showed up here today.

BRANDON

Oh shit. I'm sure that went well.

DYLAN

LOL omg, I wish I could have seen the look on her face when she saw Daphne.

ME

It wasn't that bad, actually. Daphne handled it like an adult. Courtney whined and pleaded but left without too much of a hassle.

BRANDON

So what's the issue now?

ME

I really like Daphne. Like, I really like her and I think I fucked up trying to push the whole friends-with-benefits thing. I need to tell her how I feel.

DYLAN

You've known this girl for like 30 seconds. How about you take a breath before you go professing your love to a total stranger?

BRANDON

I can't believe I'm saying this, but I have to agree with Dylan here. I know I said before maybe it was worth exploring, but telling her you have feelings for her after a couple of days seems a little weird.

ME

Mom and Dad knew after one date.

The pause in their texts told me I had struck a nerve, but it was true. Dad always said he knew she was the one. I never felt that with Courtney, but I thought our relationship would get there over time. And while I'm not saying I'm head over heels for Daphne, I do have strong feelings for her and I can definitely see a future with her if we could get out of our own way.

BRANDON

You're comparing this to Mom and Dad? That's bold.

ME

I'm not saying it's the same, but I have feelings that came on FAST and I don't think I can ignore them.

DYLAN

You know, I think you're crazy. This is way too soon. I like this fuck buddies idea though. Keep that shit up.

BRANDON

Listen, brother, this is fast, but you know how you feel and if you think it's for real, then I guess you gotta do what you feel is right.

ME

Idk if this helped or not, but thanks for listening. I'm gonna go, but I'll check in with you guys soon. Dinner at Dad's when I'm back?

DYLAN

Sounds good. Love you bro.

BRANDON

Sounds good.

I threw my phone on the bed and then flung myself on it with a huff. What the fuck was I doing? What was I going to do? My chest ached at the thought of not seeing Daphne again after we left this little bubble we'd found ourselves in. I knew it was crazy, but I think my mind was made up. I had to talk to Daphne and see if she could give us a chance. We lived in the same city—we could date. If she could be open to it, we could have a real chance.

I was exhausted and turned in early with my mind made up that tomorrow I'd come clean with Daphne. I only hoped that my confession didn't totally freak her out and scare her off.

I WOKE the next day with renewed excitement. Today was the day I was going to officially shoot my shot with Daphne. The romantic dinner was planned for tonight, and I figured it would be the perfect time to tell her how I was feeling.

I went about my usual morning routine, thankful that I didn't drink enough yesterday to feel too awful. I started the coffee and then headed out for my morning run. On my run, I imagined taking Daphne to all of my favorite places and introducing her to my family. I imagined waking up next to her every day and spending holidays with her. I knew I was getting way ahead of myself, but daydreaming about what could be was exciting and made my run more bearable.

Forty minutes later, I was a sweaty mess. When I got back to the cabin, I headed straight for the shower. Daphne still hadn't come out of her room, so I had some time to take a nice, long, hot shower. As the steam surrounded me, I couldn't help but remember the last time we were in this shower together and I couldn't wait to be with her again.

After my shower, I dressed and headed out into the living area, but Daphne was still nowhere in sight. As I made my way back into the kitchen to pour myself a cup of coffee, I noticed a piece of paper on the island. My shoulders slumped and my chest ached. I knew what it was before I picked it up. Daphne was gone.

26

DAPHNE

My fight-or-flight had fully kicked in by the time I opened my eyes in the morning. I knew I had to get out of the cabin. I just couldn't think clearly in Nathan's presence. I could smell the scent of coffee coming from the kitchen, so I knew he was already awake. I peeked out from behind my door, hoping he wasn't out there, and thankfully, he wasn't. I tiptoed to his room, and he wasn't there either. That meant he was probably on a run and I had some time to get out of there.

I ran to my room and packed my bags. Was it childish that I was running away without a word? Yes. But I wasn't thinking clearly and I don't think I had since my arrival. After gathering my things, I pulled a piece of paper out of the nightstand drawer and wrote Nathan a note. It didn't feel like enough of an explanation, but it was all I could do at that moment. I wrote and rewrote it several times. Nothing I put on the paper felt right.

~~Nathan~~

~~These last few days were a lot of fun.~~
~~Thanks for letting me crash your vacation, but~~
~~I have to get back to reality.~~

~~Thanks for letting me crash your vacay.~~
~~Had a lot of fun!~~

Nathan—

Meeting you has been the highlight of my year. I never imagined I would have had so much fun on my breakup vacation, but you made me almost forget why I was here. So thank you for that. You are an incredible person, and under different circumstances, I think I could have fallen for you. Hard. But I'm nowhere near emotionally ready for more, and you made it pretty clear that you weren't either. I truly wish you the best, and I know that when you're ready, you'll make some girl the luckiest girl in the world.
xo, Daphne

Why the fuck was I crying? God, I was such a fucking mess. I ran away from my relationship with Marcus right into the arms of another man and almost fell for him too.

What a disaster. I needed to avoid all men like the plague for a while.

I popped my head out into the living room once more to make sure Nathan wasn't around. I could barely hear the sound of his shower running, so I figured the coast was clear. I quickly gathered my things, placed the note on the kitchen island, and went out the front door with tears still in my eyes.

"Hey, it's me," I sobbed when Lexi picked up my phone call. "I just left the cabin and I'm on my way back."

"What happened? I'll fucking kill him," Lexi spit.

"Nothing. I swear he didn't do anything," I hiccuped. "After we got off the phone last night, I took a bath, and while I was soaking, I realized that I needed to get out of here. Being around him was fucking with my head. Or maybe Marcus had already fucked my head up beyond repair, and I'm second-guessing everything. Either way, I need some time alone. You know, like how this week was *supposed* to go."

"Babe, take a breath. I'm gonna need you to calm down if you're gonna drive home right now. Otherwise, pull over until you can lock that shit down. I need you to get home in one piece." Lexi sounded worried, so I did my best to collect myself. "Deep breaths. Everything is fine. But why are you so upset?"

"I don't know. I think I really like him, which I know is fucking crazy. Like, what if I am totally fucking up a good thing by running away? Or what if I stay and it's not a good thing, and I get stuck in yet another shitty relationship? See?

I'm all over the place. I can't stop my brain from running wild. I just had to go." I was sobbing now and decided Lexi was right. I had to pull over.

"Bitch, you'd better pull over and take a minute."

"I am." I pulled off the side of the road into a lookout area that overlooked the lake. From here, I could probably still see the cabin if I let myself look in that direction. "Lexi, what the fuck is wrong with me?"

"I think Marcus seriously did a number on you and you are second-guessing yourself and overthinking this whole situation." Lexi continued to talk, but I had stopped listening. I was too distracted by the text messages chiming in from Nathan.

NATHAN

Daphne, please come back and talk to me.

NATHAN

We need to talk about this.

NATHAN

I didn't mean what I said. I'm an idiot.

My sobbing increased and then Lexi's voice cut through, "Daphne, talk to me. What's happening?"

"Nathan is texting me. Oh shit, now he's calling. Fuck, Lex, am I doing the right thing?" I cried as I sent Nathan to voicemail.

"You're okay. We can talk about it when you get here. Just try to calm down so you get here in one piece."

"Okay. I'm okay. I'm gonna sit here for a few minutes

and then I'll be on my way." My breathing was returning to normal, and my sobbing had subsided.

"Love you, bitch. Drive safe," Lexi said before we said our goodbyes.

After I hung up the phone, I rested my forehead on the steering wheel and took some more deep breaths. My mind was racing, but I was resolute in my decision to get back to Lexi's. I needed time and space to figure out what I wanted, and unfortunately, that meant I couldn't talk to Nathan right now.

As I sat there with my forehead on the steering wheel, I heard the sound of another car on the gravel in the lookout spot. I lifted my head and squinted through my puffy, tear-soaked eyes to see Nathan's car pulling up behind me in the rear-view mirror. *Shit*.

Before I could think about putting the car into drive, Nathan was ripping my door open like a man possessed. "What the fuck, Daphne?" he boomed, looming above me with his chest heaving, arms braced across the opening of my door, caging me in.

"Hey," I said weakly. The note I left him had said what I wanted him to know, but I couldn't meet his eyes. I was not proud of how I left things, but I knew I had to leave without facing him, or I might not have had the strength to walk away from whatever this was or could be.

Nathan squatted down next to me and turned my face gently toward his. "Baby, look at me."

Tears filled my eyes again as they met Nathan's. "I'm so sorry," I sobbed into his chest as he wrapped his strong arms around me. I sat there in his arms and cried while he whispered sweet, comforting things like "It's okay" and "I've got you." Once I calmed down again, I pushed away from his chest to see the concerned look in his eyes. Great, now he thought I was fucking crazy. "I—" I started, but he interrupted me.

"Baby, listen to me. I fucked up. I let you think that this meant nothing to me. I said friends with benefits, but that's not what I wanted. Not really." He was rushing his words, trying to get it all out before I could interject. He put his hands on my face, forcing me to look at him. "I know this is crazy, but I have feelings for you that I didn't expect, and I, I…fuck, I panicked. I thought it was too soon for both of us, but I couldn't let you just leave the other day, so I said the only thing I could think of to get you to stay." His eyes darted back and forth between mine, looking desperate.

If I were in a place to accept it, his heartfelt confession would have been the most romantic moment of my life. But, instead, it fell on deaf ears. I was in a panic to get out of there, not ready for this with anyone, no matter how much I wished I was. I covered his hands with my own and slowly lowered them from my face. I held his hands in mine, studying them for a moment, and then my gaze traveled up to meet his again. He looked so hopeful, yet hopeless at the same time. It probably would've broken my heart if my heart had been whole. But the truth was, my heart was already broken, and I needed to put it back together before I could open it up to him or anyone else.

"Nathan," I started as a tear slipped out and down my cheek.

"Don't, Daphne. Please don't push me away. I know the timing is trash, but you can't tell me you don't feel this too. There's something here, and I think it's worth exploring."

"I can't. I'm not ready. My heart isn't ready for you. Please let me go," I sobbed. "I'm not saying never. I'm saying not right now."

Nathan's jaw clenched, and I could tell he was fighting the urge to argue with me. That alone was enough for me to reconsider, but I knew I had to hold firm. "Kitten, I will wait for you, but please don't shut me out completely. I couldn't bear it."

"I need time, Nathan. I still haven't fully recovered from my breakup. He really did a number on me, and then I met you, and my brain sort of short-circuited. You make it almost impossible to think straight. Has anyone ever told you that?" I chuckled.

"I can't say I've heard that before, but I'm taking it as a compliment. And like I said, I'll wait and I'll give you time, but apparently, I'm not a very patient man when it comes to you."

I gave him a small smile as I looked up at him through my damp lashes. Before I could blink, his lips crashed into mine. His kiss was ravenous and desperate and full of so many words left unsaid between us. I hoped our story wasn't over, but I kissed him as if it were goodbye, anyway. When we separated, I was breathless and so turned on I was tempted to pull him into the car to fuck me one last time.

But I knew that was not the move, and I had to get out of there before my whore of a vagina took over again.

"I've gotta go, Nathan," I said with a pout. "Just give me some time, okay?"

"Okay," he said as he reluctantly released me and stood back to his full height. "Will you please text me that you got home safe, at least?"

"I can do that. I promise." I smiled up at him. He closed my door and gave me a small wave as I put the car in drive and started the drive back to reality.

27

NATHAN

Fuck.

28

DAPHNE

I was rethinking and second-guessing everything, especially my relationship with Marcus. I knew Marcus wasn't my person, but he had my head so fucked up that I wasn't sure of anything anymore. Was any of it real? I replayed every moment of my time with Marcus and at the cabin with Nathan. The drive home felt like the longest of my life. Home. I didn't have a home anymore, did I? The home I built with Marcus wasn't mine. It was a lie. It was a placeholder. But for what?

When I did finally leave Marcus, it felt like a huge weight was lifted off me. Lexi had asked me why I stayed with him for so long, and I think it was because he made me believe I was the problem. I was the broken one who would leave perfectly fine relationships for "no reason" in the past, and so I made myself stay because he was so good at manipulating me into thinking I was the issue. But wasn't I the issue? I just ran from what could possibly have been the best man I had ever met. And for what? Because of the timing? Maybe I wasn't cut out for relationships. Maybe I was destined to be alone.

When I arrived at Lexi's place, she greeted me at the door the way she always did after a particularly hard day, with a hug and a glass of wine.

"Hey babe," she said as she squeezed me tight. "You okay?"

"No," I sobbed into her hair. "I am most definitely not okay." I squeezed her back just as hard. Lexi and I had been friends for years after meeting when she came to work in my department at the hospital. We became fast friends and have seen each other through some pretty tough situations. I loved her like she was family. Fuck, she *was* family.

I pulled myself away from her and wiped my face with my sleeve. I'm sure I looked like a total train wreck, but I didn't care, and I knew Lexi didn't care either. "I'm so glad you didn't have to work tonight. I just needed some Lexi time," I hiccuped.

"I've got you, babe. Even if I were on the schedule tonight, I would have called out for you. Let's face it though, I call out if the wind blows the wrong way," she laughed. It was true, though. Lexi had a love-hate relation-ship with work. She loved the money but hated to work. It wasn't that she hated being a nurse necessarily. More like she didn't want to work at all. But she also didn't want to be someone's trophy wife. Lexi was a complex and indepen-dent woman, and I was grateful to have her in my life.

She pushed the wine glass into my hand and ushered me

to the couch, where she had snacks already waiting for me on the coffee table. All of my favorites were there—cheese and caramel popcorn, multiple varieties of gummy candy, and beef jerky. I know, I know, a weird combo, but my favorites, nonetheless. I definitely lucked out in the bestie department.

We sat facing each other with our legs curled up on the couch and a fluffy throw blanket over us. I swallowed a big swig of wine and then took a deep breath. Lexi already knew the bulk of what was going on and I didn't particularly feel like rehashing everything, but I knew she'd give it to me straight.

"Tell me I'm doing the right thing."

"I'm not you, Daphne," she winced. "I'm not a relationship girl, so I couldn't say. I would have left, but not for the same reasons you did." She was right, of course. Lexi didn't do relationships. She did friends with benefits, one-night stands, and situationships, whatever that meant.

"Yeah, I know that, but I guess I need some reassurance that I'm not crazy for walking out on something that could have been something because it felt too soon, ya know?"

"You are not crazy. Period," Lexi said definitively. "You are emotional and impulsive sometimes, but not crazy. If you felt like it was too soon to start something with the sex god, then it was too soon. Take some time and get your head right, and then you can reevaluate."

"But what if I fucked this up beyond repair? What if I decide I was wrong, but Nathan's already moved on when I reach out? I'm freaking out, Lexi. I feel like I'm always leaving relationships or potential relationships. What if I'm the problem?"

"You listen to me and you listen good. You are not the problem, bitch. Your feelings are valid. Marcus fucked with your head for far too long, and you need some time to get your mind right. I fully support your taking a break and doing just that." Lexi sounded so sure of what she said that I almost believed her, even if the voice in the back of my mind was still unsure.

We continued to chat and eat and drink, and I was just starting to feel a little calmer when my phone buzzed in my bag. Lexi gave me a knowing look. It was one of three people. Marcus, Nathan, or my mom, whom I had still yet to tell about my situation. It wasn't that I wasn't close with my mom, I was, but she was also a huge fan of Marcus and I hadn't been looking forward to that particular conversation. I huffed, made an exaggerated show of getting up, and rolled my eyes as I stalked over to my bag that I had left by the entryway.

Fucking Marcus. Of course, it was him *again*. He was really getting on my nerves, so I decided I was going to give him a piece of my mind this time. "What?" I snapped as I answered his call.

"Hey babe," he slurred his words as if he'd been drinking. "I've missed you so much. When are you coming home?"

"You're delusional, Marcus. I broke up with you and moved out, remember?" I quipped.

"Daph, there's no way we're over. I love you, and we're

so good together. I miss you so much. Just come home and we can sort this all out." Marcus must have really believed his own bullshit. How could he think I'd come back, especially after all the unhinged messages he'd sent me over the past week?

"Marcus, we are done. I'm not coming back. I do not miss you. Please stop calling me." I sighed. He was so exhausting, and I was over this conversation. "Goodbye, Marcus."

I hung up the phone and immediately blocked Marcus on everything. I was done dealing with the constant texts and calls. I don't know why I hadn't done it sooner. As I went to put my phone down, it chimed with an incoming text. It was Nathan checking to make sure I got home okay. I let out a slow exhale as I stared at my phone. Shit, I totally forgot that I promised to let him know I got in safe. I tapped out a quick reply that I was fine and then turned my phone off completely. I needed bestie time without distractions of the male variety.

29

NATHAN

My plan had completely backfired, and Daphne left anyway. I knew it was probably too soon for both of us to get involved with each other, but I also couldn't deny the pull we shared. I was drawn to her immediately, and our chemistry was something I'd never felt before, not even with the woman I was supposed to marry. Crazy, huh? I was sure that Daphne felt it too, and that's why she ran. It scared her to feel for me so soon after her breakup, and I couldn't blame her in the slightest. I was completely surprised by my feelings too, but I wasn't willing to let her walk away from this without telling her how I felt.

As I watched her car pull out onto the road and drive out of sight, I was uncertain if I'd ever see her again, but I swore I'd do everything in my power to make sure that I did. She wanted space, and I could respect that. For now.

The short drive back to the cabin was filled with silence —my thoughts were all over the place. Was I doing the right thing? Had I just lost her? Would I see her again? Would she block my number and move on completely? Would she want to explore things with me in the future? God, I was going to drive myself crazy.

When I reached the cabin and went inside, it seemed colder despite the fire that I had left burning in the fireplace. One thing was clear: I needed to get the fuck out of this cabin. There was no way I wanted to be here without Daphne. I wanted to surround myself with my family. They always brightened my mood, even if they sometimes drove me nuts. But first, I had to cancel the dinner I had planned for tonight and let the cabin owner know I was checking out early. This day was totally fucked and turned out nothing like I had planned or hoped it would.

After canceling the dinner and contacting the cabin owner, I packed up my things and left. I drove right to my dad's from the cabin and called him to make sure he'd be around. Of course, he told me to come right over. It was reassuring that I could always count on him and my brothers, no matter what.

My childhood home was just outside the city and a couple of hours from the cabin. During the drive, Daphne consumed my thoughts. Taking in the sights on the way, I was reminded of how much Daphne loved the changing leaves and the scenery when we drove into town that first day. That day was perfect. We laughed and joked, and things were so easy between us. To think I may not get to experience days like that again with her was too much to bear.

As I got closer to my dad's place, my spiraling thoughts shifted to fond memories of my family. My childhood was a happy one filled with loving and supportive parents. My parents were the epitome of what a relationship should be and when we lost my mom a few years back, it took a toll on all of us. I will forever be grateful for the life she gave us and the example she and my dad set for us.

The house I grew up in was a modest two-story colonial on a quiet street lined with mature trees that were starting to change color and lose their leaves for the season. It was such a cozy neighborhood that you couldn't tell it was so close to the city. We grew up riding our bikes up and down the street, staying out from morning till night, playing with neighbor kids, and generally causing a ruckus. Our parents had their hands full with the three of us, but I suspect they wouldn't have changed a thing.

As I pulled into the driveway, I noticed my brother Brandon's car was also there. Good. I could use some brother time too. I parked and walked up to the front door. Before I could reach the handle, my dad was there, opening it and ushering me inside. He brought me into a bear hug and slapped my back. "How's my boy?" he boomed. I was a big guy, but my dad was a beast and, according to some regulars at the shop, a silver fox. He stood 6'5" and was almost double as broad as me.

I groaned and chuckled, "I was fine until you just crushed my spine, so thanks for that, Pops."

"Pussy," he laughed under his breath. "Come on in. Your brothers are here too."

"Is that lover boy?" Dylan called from the kitchen. Great, they weren't gonna take it easy on me.

"Lover boy?" my dad questioned. "I thought you and whore bag broke up?"

"Jesus, Dad, whore bag? Tell me what you really think." I shook my head as we entered the kitchen, or as Mom used to call it, Grand Central Station. This kitchen was the epicenter of the house. It was where we ate all our meals, did our homework, and usually congregated while we were growing up.

"Son, she's a cheater, and you know how I feel about that shit. That's unforgivable. So yeah, her new name is whore bag," he laughed, giving me another thump on the shoulder.

"Fair enough, and yes, we broke up. Her cheating was most definitely a deal breaker for me," I agreed. "Hey Brandon, hey Dylan," I greeted my brothers, giving them each a hug. After saying our hellos, Brandon grabbed some beers from the fridge and passed one to each of us.

"What brings you home so soon? Trouble in paradise already?" Dylan asked with a grin. Fucking asshole.

"What's that about?" Dad asked, "Seriously, what's going on?"

I sighed heavily and then filled him in on my beautiful surprise at the cabin, the PG version of the events that unfolded and how she went running for the hills.

"Wow, you've had some week, son." My dad grimaced. "So what now?"

Brandon chimed in, "Have you talked to her since she left?"

"Oh, shit no. She was supposed to text me when she got home, but I haven't heard from her yet." I pulled my phone out and shot off a quick text to ask if she had made it home safe.

Ding. She replied almost immediately.

DAPHNE

Yeah, I'm good. Thanks.

Ouch. But at least she responded, so I wouldn't worry. I tapped out another message.

ME

Okay, good. I meant what I said, Baby. I want to explore this, whatever this is, but I know you need time. I want to respect that, but idk how long I'll last. If nothing else, please don't shut me out completely, okay?

Nothing. Not even a read receipt. She either put her phone down or turned it off. My brows furrowed. "Shit," I said as I pocketed my phone.

"That good, huh?" Brandon bumped his shoulder into mine, drawing my attention back to the group.

"Yeah, she said she needed space, but I can't seem to let that happen. I think I fucked up today when I went after her." I thought back to the look in her eyes on the side of the road as I told her how I felt. Did I say too much? Did I completely overwhelm her?

"Hey, at least she knows where you stand, bro. And if you have real feelings for her, you have to lay it all out there for her. Give her all the facts so she can make an informed decision." Out of my brothers, Brandon was definitely the optimist when it came to love and relationships, though he himself had been unlucky in love as of yet.

"Jesus. Do you hear yourself?" Dylan scoffed. "He just met the girl. It's not like she's the love of his life or something."

At that, Dad chimed in, "What have I always said? When you know, you know. I knew from the moment I met your mother that she was it for me. Sometimes it happens that way. Don't give your brother shit just because the only pussy you've ever loved is your fucking cat." That did it. Brandon and I were dead. I was bent over, clutching my stomach, laughing my ass off.

Dylan looked offended, although I doubt he was. "You leave my Coco Baby out of this!" Dylan roared.

God, I loved these ding-dongs. They made everything a little more bearable.

"All right, all right," Dad started. "You all staying for dinner? I'm making Mom's chicken parm."

Hell yes, I was staying for dinner.

Dinner was delicious, and it felt so good to be in the company of my dad and brothers again. The weeks leading up to what would have been my wedding were hectic, to say the least, and aside from our tux fittings, I hadn't gotten to hang out with them. It probably didn't help that they weren't exactly card-carrying members of the Courtney

Taylor Fan Club. I guess they saw what I should have all along, that Courtney was a self-absorbed, fame-hungry waste of my time. Thankfully, I didn't hear any more "I told you sos" over dinner and we spent the time catching up on what had been going on in their lives.

For the most part, it was the same old, same old, but Dad had alluded that he was coming back to work at the shop. I guess being retired didn't suit him, and he was bored out of his mind. My brothers were, of course, delighted for him to come back. Although they'd still run the place, our dad was eager to get back to tattooing again and rejoin the fun in the shop. Since Mom's death a few years back, he'd retreated from the world, and we were excited to see him starting to get back to his old self. I knew he'd never completely get over losing Mom, but it was still nice to see him making progress.

After dinner, we went into the sunroom for a nightcap, which was our usual after-dinner routine. We used to do this when Mom was around too, staying together in each other's company a little while longer before we headed back to our places. "So, what do you plan to do about Daphne?" Brandon asked as we all got settled into our seats.

"Honestly, right now, I don't know. I feel like I should give her the space she asked for, but I'm afraid that if I do, I'll lose her," I sighed, thinking back to her face before I closed her back into her car. She looked so sad, like she really didn't want space from me, but what was I supposed to do? Force her to stay?

"Yeah, you're in a bit of a tough situation, son. If she's

as special as you say, you'll work it out. Don't give up." Dad was an eternal romantic despite the heartache he'd experienced.

Brandon chimed in, "Yeah, don't give up, brother. You've got to woo her."

"Woo her?" Dylan practically choked. "You guys are wild. You met her what, like five days ago? I think you're still a little cum drunk. There's no way you have real feelings after five fucking days."

"Hey, language!" Dad scolded. Even though he had a mouth like a sailor and never censored himself, he still didn't like us to curse around him, despite the fact we were all grown men.

"Seriously, Dad? You made a pretty foul crack about me and my cat before dinner."

"Do as I say, not as I do, wiseass." Dad folded his arms over his chest, signaling that the conversation was over.

"Listen, guys, there was just something about her, and it wasn't just the S. E. X." I spelled the last word for dramatic effect. My dad was not amused and rolled his eyes at me to let me know.

Brandon continued, "Yes, woo her. You're a romance author for crying out loud. I'm sure you can come up with some sort of grand gesture to win her over."

He's right. I'd written so many grand gestures and happily ever afters. Surely, I could come up with a way to get the girl.

30

DAPHNE

My head was pounding. I really needed to lay off the booze. After I hung up the phone with Marcus, I was on a mission to forget. To forget about Marcus, to forget about Nathan, and to forget about all the things that were looming over me at the moment. Like, where was I going to live? How would I tell my parents what happened? Could I avoid Marcus completely at work?

Ugh. I rolled over on Lexi's couch and peeled my eyes open. The blaring sunlight shot directly into my eyes through the open living room curtains. Yeah, this was not going to work long-term, but it was still nice to be under the same roof as my bestie. I craved her support now more than ever, although I definitely couldn't continue to drink like that every day.

After I extricated myself from the couch, I made my way into Lexi's room and collapsed on the bed next to her.

She grunted. Her displeasure at being disturbed was clear. "Why, bitch, why? It's too fucking early," she whined.

"Yeah, well next time, don't leave me on the couch with the shades open. I think I'm blind," I joked, nudging her in the ribs. "Anyway, we're up now. Let's go get some breaky."

"Ugh, why do you hate me?" She rolled over and buried her head under her pillow. "Fiiiine, but you're buying." She eventually relented and dragged her ass to the bathroom to start the process of getting ready.

While she was busy, I started some coffee, which I immediately regretted since it made me think of the last few mornings with Nathan. Great, now freaking coffee was ruined for me. What's next? The things he did to my body and the way he made me feel, I'd never felt like that with anyone else. Did he ruin sex for me, too? *Perfect.*

I was standing in front of the coffeemaker, lost in thought, when Lexi came up behind me. "You okay?" she asked as she put a hand on my arm, startling me.

"Fuck Lexi, don't do that," I gasped. "Yeah, I'm fine. Just thinking." I poured us each a coffee. "I'll go get ready, and then we can get out of here. I'm starving." My stomach growled as if on cue.

The twenty-four-hour diner down the street from Lexi's was our favorite place in the city. We'd go there at all hours, before work, after work, after the bars, and in the mornings for breakfast on a day off. Max's Diner was not only a favorite of ours, but at any given time, you could find one or more of our coworkers popping in to grab a coffee or a meal since it was also close to the hospital. Thankfully, the one person who I could almost guarantee I wouldn't see was Marcus. Max's was beneath him, I guessed, but that was perfectly okay with me. He's the last person I wanted to deal with.

Max greeted us as we walked in, as usual. I often wondered if this woman ever slept or if she even had a home away from the diner. She seemed to always be there, but she never seemed annoyed by that fact. She was always pleasant and welcoming, although I'd seen her hold her own when the late-night crowd would get rowdy and she had to intervene.

"Hey, girls. Just the two of you today?" she asked, waving two menus in our direction.

"Yeah, Max, thanks." I nodded and followed her to a booth by the windows.

"Coffees?" Were we that predictable?

"You know it," Lexi chimed in as I examined the menu, as if I'd order anything but my usual. Max's had the best shit on a shingle in the city, and there wasn't a chance in hell I'd order anything else. Max returned with our drinks, took our orders, and then retreated to the kitchen.

"Okay, first things first." I cleared my throat. "I need to find a place to live. As much as I appreciate staying with you, I can't sleep on your couch forever. I want something close, though. If I could walk to work and to your place, that would be ideal."

"Yeah, I need you to stay close. I didn't like Marcus's place. It was too far." Lexi pouted.

"Too far? It was like a ten-minute drive."

Lexi laughed, "Yeah, I hate driving. That's why I live close to work, duh."

"I definitely want to stay close, but I may have to be open to…" My eyes bulged and my words caught in my throat. Lexi immediately caught on and whipped her head around to see what I was looking at.

"Oh hell no," she shot, narrowing her eyes as she stared at Dr. Marcus Fuckface Williams standing by the host stand. He lifted his eyes, looked right at me, and then started heading our way. What in the actual fuck? I couldn't remember a single time in our entire relationship that I had seen him here. I guess that was just my fucking luck.

He approached with a wide grin, "Hey babe, I've missed you." He leaned in and tried to kiss my cheek, which I dodged. This guy was either totally delulu or thought I'd go along with his charade so as not to cause a scene in public. He was dead ass wrong.

I pushed him gently out of my personal space as I caught sight of Lexi's gaping mouth and eye twitching. She was about to lose her shit. "Marcus, what are you doing here?" I asked calmly.

"I was heading to get lunch down the street and saw you guys walk in here. I haven't seen you, so I thought I'd pop in to say hi," he said casually as if he didn't know we had broken up.

I reached out and grabbed Marcus's arm to make sure I had his attention, as I said, "Listen, Marcus, we broke up. Please, leave me alone."

He leaned in. "No, you listen, we *are not* done. You're clearly going through something here and I've been *trying* to be supportive," he said through gritted teeth while I swear I saw Lexi's left pupil blow.

Lexi's restraint had evaporated and as she was pushing up to stand, Max arrived at the table with our food. "Everything okay here, girls?" she asked, looking warily between Marcus and us.

"Yeah, thanks, Max. Marcus was just leaving. Right, Marcus?" I said, narrowing my eyes at him.

Max, Lexi, and I all stared blankly at Marcus for a moment while he regained his composure and straightened. "Of course. I'll let you get back to your girl time. I'll see you later, babe." He smiled brightly as if we weren't just in an awkward standoff and then turned on his heel to walk out of the diner.

"You girls need anything else?" Max asked as she placed our food in front of us. I'm sure she was more concerned about our safety than if we needed ketchup. By the way, who uses ketchup at breakfast? Sociopaths like Marcus, that's who.

"We're good, Max, thanks." I smiled up at her, and she trotted off to help another table.

"The fucking balls on that guy. Seriously, like, is he okay?" Lexi shook her head and dug into her stuffed French toast.

"Yeah, that was so weird. Do you think he followed us? Or are you buying that story about being in the neighborhood for lunch?"

"There's not a chance this was a coincidence. He's out of his mind if he thinks playing dumb and pretending you're still a couple is going to get you back. Right?" She winced at the last part as if she didn't mean to let the question slip.

"Really, Lexi? Am I so pathetic that you think I'd go back to him?" I could feel myself getting upset. I knew I was a mess, but the fact that she had to check if I was considering going back to him had me questioning myself.

"No, babe, but he manipulated you for years, and I'm just checking to see where your head's at. You're not pathetic, and it wasn't your fault that you fell for his shit before. He's good at what he does." Lexi eyed me sympathetically.

"Ugh, I hate this." I pushed my beloved plate of SOS away and put my head down on the table. "Why can't he just leave me alone? Every text and voicemail sets me off, and now he's showing up randomly," I muttered with my face still on the table.

"First off," Lexi pushed my face up off the table, "please, for the love of my French toast, get your head off the table. I'm still eating here. And second, forget about that dickhead. I'm more interested in the new guy." She winked at me. The bitch actually winked at me.

I sat back in the booth, slouched down, and let out an exasperated sigh. "Nathan doesn't need my drama. He's a nice guy, and we had a great time, but emotionally I'm a total mess, and I need to sort out my own shit before I think about dragging someone else into my life." But boy, did I miss him. Who would've thought that after spending just five days with someone, I'd feel such a strong connection? But then again, that was so me, wasn't it? Bebopping from relationship to relationship and always picking the wrong guy. Whether Nathan was a great guy or yet another in a long line of mistakes, it didn't matter. I was clearly not capable of making good decisions, and I wasn't about to drag anyone else down with me.

31

NATHAN

Thankfully, Daphne was pretty easy to find online and her social media accounts weren't private. Listen, I wouldn't say I was *stalking* her. More like doing some light private investigating. I mean, how would I woo her if I didn't know where she was or what she was up to? It's not like she was giving me much to go on over text and besides, I had a plan.

Step one, recon. I needed intel. I wanted to know as much about Daphne as I possibly could. I already knew some basic things. She sucked at the game Operation, preferred red wine over white, liked to read romance novels, loved fall, Halloween, and scary movies, Italian food was her favorite, especially pizza, had an affinity for all things pumpkin spice, and thankfully lived in the same city as me. From my brief gleaning of her socials, I got a pretty clear snapshot of her life. She was a dedicated and caring nurse, volunteered at an animal shelter, and hardly went anywhere without her best friend, Lexi.

Step two was a little more complicated, and I'd need to enlist help for that. That's why the recon was so important. I had to find out who my potential allies could be. The number one contender was Lexi. As Daphne's best friend, she was an obvious choice, but I wasn't sure she'd be on board to help me get the girl. I'd have to have a pretty compelling argument to win her over, but that was a later problem.

It had been a few days since Daphne left the cabin and I hadn't heard from her since she let me know she had gotten home safe. I texted her once a day later to see how she was, but she didn't respond. She had asked for space, and I was trying my best to honor her request. I knew it was what she thought she needed, but was it what she actually needed? I wasn't so sure.

Daphne hadn't posted anything on her socials since she was at the cabin, so I wasn't entirely sure of what she was up to, but I was also checking Lexi's and happened to catch a couple of posts that indicated Daphne was staying with her. I spent the week after I returned from the cabin going between my investigative work and writing because, let's face it, regular life had to go on. Writing was going surprisingly well, despite the ever-present distraction that was Daphne, who kept invading my thoughts. Maybe she was my new muse.

After a week of radio silence, I decided to shoot my shot and sent Lexi a message through social media. We weren't friends, so I wasn't sure if she'd see it, but I hoped she would and I hoped she'd be open to helping me.

ME

Hey Lexi—I know this is totally out of left field, but I had to try something. I know we haven't officially met and I'm sorry that our first encounter is this creepy message on social media, but

Delete, delete, delete.

ME

Hey Lexi—Remember me? I shared a cabin with your good friend Daphne last week

Delete, delete, delete.

God, why was this so difficult? I felt awkward as fuck messaging this girl who I didn't even know. Finding the right words seemed impossible.

ME

Lexi—I'm in love with your best friend and I need your help.

Full send.

32

DAPHNE

My run-in with Marcus at the diner had totally rattled me. I spent the next week and a half going to and from work and taking up residence on Lexi's couch. Work was fucking wild. I don't know if it was a full moon or something, but we were busy as shit. In the past three days alone, we had several codes in the unit, even more on the floors and what felt like a bazillion admissions. I barely left the unit, and I was able to avoid Marcus, although I saw him occasionally while walking in or out of the building. I chalked it up to coincidence and nothing more, since he hadn't tried to corner me again.

Lexi had to have been so sick of my shit because she was constantly trying to get me to go out with her and get me to leave my new favorite place, her couch. I didn't want to do anything. I was miserable. Nathan occupied most of my thoughts. I missed him so much. I knew that, yet I still thought it best to keep my distance, even if it meant making myself suffer.

Nathan deserved a whole-ass person, not someone who was as fucked up as I was. My brain kept telling me that I was the problem, though Lexi kept telling me I wasn't. Okay, then why hadn't I told my parents about the breakup yet? Why had every relationship I'd ever been in been so similar? There were two reasons for that—I had a type (assholes), and I was too quick to jump in before I knew the person. While I didn't think Nathan was an asshole, I also didn't trust my judgment since, once again, I had jumped in before I really knew the guy. But I didn't jump in. I got the fuck out before any real feelings could develop. Didn't I?

I didn't have to wonder if he was thinking about me, though, because he had *somehow* gotten my address and had been sending me little things to make sure I knew I was on his mind too. Fucking Lexi. She denied being involved, but I knew she had something to do with him getting her address. Every few days, something new would show up for me. Flowers, home-cooked chicken parm, the game Operation, a collection of scary movies on DVD, a fluffy blanket that was eerily similar to my favorite one from the cabin. Everything he sent brought back memories of our time together, and each gift came with its own heartfelt note. He wanted more, and I was just blowing him off. God, what was wrong with me?

I was deep in thought when Lexi came practically skipping into the room. I was laid out on the couch in two-day-old jammies, with chip pieces trailing down my shirt, and my hair definitely could use a brush run through it. She scrunched up her nose at me. "Jesus, Daphne, you look like shit."

"Oh thanks, love you too," I shot back, rolling my eyes. I knew I looked like shit, but I'd be damned if I was going to take her insult lying down. Well, I was still lying down, but I wasn't just gonna take it.

"Seriously, babe, I can't take it anymore. You've been holed up on my couch for days, being a total sad sack. You need to get out and stop feeling sorry for yourself." She stood in front of the TV with her arms crossed over her chest.

"I'm not feeling sorry for myself. I'm sad, and I'm not ready to pretend I'm happy yet. Sorry if my emotions aren't working on your timeline." I rolled myself over on the couch so I didn't have to look her in the eyes. Lexi had a way of seeing through my bullshit, and I knew she wasn't going to leave me alone until she got to the real issue at hand, and I wasn't ready to admit to her or myself that I was missing Nathan.

"Look, there's a Halloween party tomorrow night at this club and I need my wing woman. Please don't make me miss it just to sit here and watch you become one with my couch." Although I couldn't see her, I knew she was pouting and giving me puppy-dog eyes. "P…p…p…please, Daphs! You love all this Halloween stuff and it'll be so fun!"

I turned back over and found her on her knees, hands

clasped together over her chest, begging me. I rolled my eyes again. "God, you're so annoying."

She knew she had me, and I hated that I gave in so easily to her. She actually squealed and threw herself at me. "Oh my God, thank you! You're the bestest friend a girl could ask for!" She squeezed so tightly, eliciting a small chuckle from me.

"Whatever. You owe me." I huffed, "Now let me get back to my self-wallowing or whatever."

"Nope. We need costumes for this shindig! I'm thinking sexy nurses! Whatcha think?" she asked hopefully, but I only hoped she was kidding.

"Not a chance in hell. That's so fucking cliché." If I rolled my eyes anymore, they might have gotten stuck there. "I will go as literally anything else, but you couldn't pay me to go as a nurse."

"Fiiine. How about sexy clowns?"

"Why does every costume you ever suggest start with the word sexy?" I sighed, knowing I was going to give in to her. "Fine. Sexy clowns it is, but please make them cute. I swear if I have a fake red nose and big yellow shoes, I will not leave this house."

Lexi jumped up, looking more excited than was necessary for the win. I guess it was the least I could do after she let me stay with her while I figured out my next moves, which have been put on the back burner this week. I had lost my motivation to find a place after our run-in with Marcus, and I was glad she wasn't pushing me to leave quite yet. It was nice to be here with her while my brain was such a mess. I think if I had been on my own, I would've been worse off, and I definitely wouldn't be going out to a party at a club. Fuck, what did I get myself into?

The next day, Lexi presented me with the most ridiculous costumes imaginable. I glared with thin lips at the pile of colorful tulle on her bed as she stood by with arms spread and a huge smile. "Ta-da!"

"You've got to be joking." I was not amused. This colorful array of fabrics did not match my mood in the slightest, and I wasn't sure how it would all come together to make a costume. It looked like a mess.

"I am not kidding. Just give it a chance, okay? I promise we are going to look so good when I'm done!" Her smile was so wide and so sincere that I had no choice but to go along with her plan. I only hoped I didn't look too crazy when we left the apartment. I was a fan of Halloween, not looking like a crazy person in public.

She started with our hair and makeup, and she did an amazing job. It wasn't giving *clown* clown, it was more like clown chic. Pale skin but not stark white, blue, and purple eye makeup, with perfect red lips and circles of red on our noses and cheeks. For our hair, she had found us some fun-colored wigs—purple for her and neon green for me. I hated to admit it, but we looked really good so far, and I was feeling more like myself. Maybe this *would* be fun.

Next up was that pile of mismatched tulle. As she tossed different pieces in my direction, I wasn't sure how it would all come together, but I decided to trust the process and let Lexi dress me. There were thigh-high blue fishnets, followed by a frilly pink corset and a bright blue neck ruffle, and last, a purple tulle tutu that did not even cover my ass. Thankfully, she let me put on some opaque boy shorts underneath it. After everything was in place and she was satisfied with the final look, she led me into the bathroom to look at her handiwork.

"Whoa!" I gasped as I looked at myself in the mirror. "This looks good, Lex. I'm impressed."

"Told ya. I can make anything look sexy, even a clown." She grinned back at me, obviously proud of herself. "Now go make us a drink while I get in my outfit."

I did as instructed and made us a couple of cocktails while she finished getting ready. When she stepped out of her room, she looked amazing. A mirror image of me, but in different colors. We looked hot, and I was starting to actually get excited about our night out. Although I wasn't interested in the attention we were sure to get from the opposite sex. I knew Lexi craved that, so I was happy to be her wing woman for the night. I mean, it was the least I could do since I had been a pretty poor house guest over the past couple of weeks.

"Damn, Lex, you did a great job putting these together. We look great!" I said as I handed her a drink. "Cheers!"

"Cheers, bitch!" She smiled and took a sip of her drink. "We should leave soon. I'll order us an Uber."

Our ride was a few short minutes away, so we downed our drinks and headed outside to wait. As I stepped out onto the sidewalk, I had that eerie feeling where you think someone is watching you, so I spun my head around to look to my right in time to see someone turn on a dime and walk in the opposite direction. They were too far away for me to tell who it was or if they had been looking our way, but something felt off. I tried to shake off the feeling and focus on our night ahead. I'm sure it was just my mind playing tricks on me or that drink that I drank entirely too fast.

33

NATHAN

Brandon had a shit-eating grin on his face as we entered the club. Great, he was loving this a little too much. I thought he'd be the safer option of my two brothers to come along with me, but I was beginning to rethink my choice. Brandon was a workaholic and rarely went out to a club, but for me, he made an exception. Let me rephrase: he did it, as he put it, for the wooing.

My brother, Brandon, a giant bear of a man with tattoos from chin to ankle, was a hopeful romantic. Dylan was a player, and I was the relationship guy. I knew if I invited Dylan, he would've bailed on me the moment he spotted his next conquest, whereas Brandon was in it for the plot. He wanted me to get the girl, and he wanted to be the one to help. I'd never hear the end of this from Dylan, though. He thought this was the dumbest idea I'd ever had, even though it wasn't my idea but Lexi's.

When I sent that message to her, I didn't know how or if

she'd respond, but I was pleasantly surprised when I heard from her a couple of days later. I explained that I really wanted to give things a go with her friend and asked if she thought Daphne could be open to it, though she had been shutting me out. Lexi told me that Daphne had been miserable and moping around, probably missing me, but was too stubborn to admit it. It surprised me that she confessed that, but I assumed she just had Daphne's best interest at heart and wanted to help lift her friend's sour mood. Lexi gave me her address so I could send Daphne a few things to hopefully soften her toward me. Then, when Lexi mentioned she had planned to go to this Halloween party and could probably coerce Daphne into going too, I decided I could "bump into her" there and shoot my shot again.

So there we were, walking into a Halloween party at a busy nightclub, me in a *Scream* mask and Brandon in a Jason mask. We kind of phoned it in on the costume front, each wearing all black and our masks, but I wasn't here for the costumes, the party, or anything else but to hopefully strike up a conversation with Daphne. I was sure if I could get in front of her, things would progress naturally, just like they had in the cabin.

Brandon and I wedged ourselves into the closest bar and ordered a couple of drinks—a bourbon for me and a beer for him. I turned, placing my back to the bar, lifted my mask to the top of my head, and took a long sip of my drink. My gaze swept the perimeter of the dance floor, and I watched the door every time it opened to admit another partygoer. I was halfway through my drink when they walked through the door. Lexi had loosely told me what they'd be wearing so I could recognize them when they came in. Never in a million years would I have guessed that I would have a thing for clowns, yet here I was, slack-jawed, eye-fucking the sexiest damn clown I had ever seen.

I would've spotted Daphne even if Lexi hadn't told me they'd be dressed as clowns. I would know that body anywhere. Her thick thighs and that juicy ass of hers were on full display, and all I wanted to do was hoist her over my shoulder and run out of there with her before anyone else got a look at her. Instead, I lowered my mask and watched her.

She and Lexi made their way to the far side of the room to another bar. Several men who were obviously trying to buy them drinks immediately surrounded them. Lexi waved them off while Daphne was looking around, almost nervously. I kept my focus on her. Could she feel my eyes on her?

"Hey, is that them?" Brandon tipped his head in their direction as he nudged my side with his elbow. He had laughed when I told him to be on the lookout for sexy clowns, but he wasn't laughing now. He looked as enthralled as I was, but his gaze was directed at Lexi. Hmm. I'd have to circle back to that later because Daphne was now staring at me, staring at her from across the room. Even through my mask, our eyes seemed to lock onto one another. It was as if she knew it was me.

"That's her," I said to my brother without taking my eyes off Daphne, and I pushed off the bar and made my way across the room. Daphne started toward me too, and we met in the middle of the now-busy dance floor.

"Are you following me?" she asked when we were about a foot apart, peering up at me with skeptical eyes and a stern look.

I lifted my mask with a smirk and she gasped, "Nathan? What are you doing here?" She looked completely surprised. I think she really thought I was someone who had followed her.

My smile was gone. "Someone was following you? What happened?" If she thought someone had followed her, what the hell was she doing confronting them?

"No, no, I thought I saw someone at the apartment, but I guess I imagined it." She shook her head as if she were trying to shake off the memory. Then her beautiful, orbit-changing smile returned, and she directed it straight into my soul. "What are you doing here?"

"Come with me," I said as I took her by the hand and guided her off the dance floor and into a quieter corner so we could talk. When I had her all to myself, I leaned in, my mouth inches from her ear. "I had to see you."

She pulled away to look me in the eye. "How did you… ahh, fucking Lexi." She shook her head and smiled. "I thought it was weird how much effort she put into these costumes and how she *insisted* I come out tonight. You two are quite the team." She leveled me with a fake look of displeasure, but I knew better. She was happy to see me, and I hoped that we could pick things up where we left off, or at least start again.

"Don't blame her. I'm not too proud to admit that I've been pretty desperate to see you, so I enlisted her help. I basically begged her."

"I'm sure it took a lot of convincing," she laughed. "Honestly, I've been a bit of a sad sack these past couple of weeks, but getting your special deliveries helped brighten my mood. I'm sorry I haven't reached out to thank you."

"I'm glad I could help your mood and there's no need to thank me. I just wanted you to know I was thinking about you. I hope you don't mind." I winced.

"Not at all. I've been thinking a lot about you, too." She nervously looked down at her feet. "I should've called or texted, but I'm still sorting out some things and didn't want to drag you into my drama." She stared down at her hands, not meeting my eyes.

I reached out and cupped her face in my hands and lifted her chin so she was gazing into my eyes, "Baby, you could drag me into anything, and I'd gladly follow."

The smile she gave me was so bright and so genuine, and it brought me right back to our first meeting in the cabin. Then she lifted onto her toes and kissed me on my cheek. Not where I wanted it, but I'd take whatever she was willing to give. A high-top table nearby opened up, so we grabbed it and then spent some time catching up. We chatted as if no time had passed, the conversation flowing as easily as before.

"Shit, I wonder if Lexi is okay. I totally forgot I was supposed to be her wing woman tonight," she said as she scanned the crowd.

"I wouldn't worry about her. I asked Brandon to keep her company while we caught up." And by the way Brandon had been checking her out before, I was sure it wasn't going to be much of a burden.

"Your brother has no idea what he agreed to, my friend. Lexi is a lot," she giggled and then pushed back in her chair. "I'll be right back. I'm just going to run to the bathroom."

She practically bounced out of sight on her way to the back of the club, and I watched her every move with a grin plastered on my face. I was so fucked.

34

DAPHNE

I was practically skipping to the bathroom, I was so happy. I couldn't believe Nathan was here, and that he had conspired with Lexi to surprise me. I didn't think I was ready to see him, yet those doubts evaporated as soon as I did. I felt so at ease with him, especially when I saw him in that mask with his tight-fitting black tee. Oh, sweet baby Cheesus did he look good. I was surprised I only kissed his cheek. If we hadn't been in a busy nightclub, I probably would've dropped to my knees right then and there.

I rounded a corner near the back of the club to find the bathrooms when I was pulled roughly by my arm. I whipped my head around to see a snarling Marcus with a death grip on my wrist. "What the fuck do you think you're doing, Daphne?" He looked completely unhinged. His face reddened, his breathing was labored, and his eyes were almost black. I had never seen him so mad before.

I swallowed, but my throat was so dry. "Marcus…did

you…follow…" I was cut off as he dragged me into a darkened corner and slammed me against the wall, knocking the air out of my lungs.

"Shut the fuck up. I have played nice and let you have your space, but this is getting ridiculous, Daphne. You need to come home. Tonight." He spat the words at me, each one coming out laced with venom as he squeezed tighter on my wrist.

"Please stop, Marcus. You're hurting me," I begged and tried in vain to pull out of his grasp.

"Hurting you? What do you think you're doing to me? Blocking my calls? Going out dressed like a whore, throwing yourself at other men." He moved his other hand to my throat, and that's when panic truly set in. I needed to get the fuck away from him. He didn't press hard enough to hurt me, but his warning was received loud and clear. Tears pricked at my eyes, but I refused to let them fall. I had cried enough because of him over the years.

I scratched at the hand on my throat and tried to wrench my other hand free from his grasp. "Marcus, please stop. I don't want to be with you." His grip on my throat tightened, making it more difficult to get the words out. "Please. Stop." A tear slipped down my cheek.

"Get your fucking hands off her," a deep voice that I would've recognized anywhere growled. Surprised by the interruption, Marcus released his grip on me as Nathan pulled him away by the back of his shirt. As Marcus's hand left my throat, I sucked in a breath and crumbled to the ground, and the tears I had been trying to hold back fell freely. Everything seemed to happen in slow motion then.

I looked up to see both men absolutely seething at one another. "Who the fuck do you think you are?" Marcus spat.

Nathan had Marcus by the collar with both hands and pulled him in close. "I'm the guy who's gonna teach you not to put your damn hands on what's mine, you piece of shit."

"Yours? You think that whore…" Marcus was cut off as Nathan punched him with a quick right hook, sending him careening back and to the ground. Shit. Marcus was stunned but not incapacitated, and Nathan was shaking his hand as if he had hurt himself too.

As if I were watching a movie, the playback seemed to speed up and then everything was happening so fast. The next thing I knew, Lexi was there in front of me on the ground, and Nathan and Marcus were being separated by another ridiculously large man in a Jason mask. A few bouncers had entered the mix, and I lost sight of Nathan as Lexi helped me up to sit in a nearby chair. Someone handed me a glass of water, and a bouncer came to check on me. I briefly told him what had happened, and that Nathan was protecting me.

What a fucking shit show. When the cops eventually came and took statements from everyone, thankfully, Marcus was the one who left the club in cuffs. The bouncers had seen Marcus accosting me, but Nathan got to him before they could, so they corroborated his story. I decided to press charges, so hopefully, Marcus would finally get the hint and leave me alone.

After the cops were done talking to me and EMS gave me a quick once-over, I was in a daze and Lexi started moving me to the exit. When we were outside, she put me in the back of a taxi and then climbed in beside me.

"Are you okay?" Lexi asked when the cab pulled away from the curb. I reached down to rub my throbbing wrist. Fuck, that hurt. Hopefully, it wouldn't leave a mark.

"Um, yeah, I'm fine. Wait, where's Nathan?" I shrugged off my internal panic to focus on someone other than myself. Typical.

"Nathan's fine. Don't worry about him. I'm more worried about you right now. Are you hurt? I should take you to the hospital to get you fully checked out," she asked as she assessed my wrist.

I cringed both at the pain in my wrist and the thought of going to the hospital. The last thing I wanted to do was go to our place of employment and rehash the sordid details of what brought me in. I was embarrassed and didn't want my coworkers to know what had happened.

"No! We don't need to go to the hospital. I'm fine, really. I just want to go home." Home. Just as I said the word, a single tear escaped and tracked down my face. The only time I'd felt at home in the last few weeks was when I was in the cabin with Nathan. How a complete stranger could evoke that feeling boggled my mind, but it was true. Nathan felt like home.

35

NATHAN

When I saw that guy with his hands on Daphne, I saw red. I'd never been a particularly jealous or violent man, but seeing Daphne being manhandled by that piece of shit made me practically homicidal. He got off lucky. If I hadn't been pulled away from him, there's no telling what I would have done. After we were ripped apart, I wanted to go straight to Daphne, but then the bouncers were there, and then the cops. It was a total cluster fuck. When I had a moment to check on Daphne, I saw her being led out the front by Lexi, so at least I knew she would be taken care of.

Once we were in Brandon's car, he turned to me and asked, "What the hell happened? I saw you and Daphne talking, and everything seemed to be going well, and the next thing I knew, there were people hollering, and you were knocking some guy out."

"He was hurting Daphne. He's lucky I didn't kill him." I was so mad I was shaking. "If she's seriously hurt, I may have to find the asshole and do just that."

"Okay, take a breath. I'm sure she's okay." Brandon started the car and headed to my place.

I was staring out of the window, clenching my fists, trying to calm down, but I was livid. I couldn't get that terrified look on her face out of my head, and the sight of his hand on her neck was seared into my memory. I needed to see her and make sure she was okay. I shot off a text to her.

ME

Hey, are you okay? Can I see you?

I didn't know if she'd respond or even look at her phone, so I quickly pulled up Lexi's number and sent her a text as well.

ME

Hey, is she okay? Where are you? I need to see her.

I was impatiently staring at my phone, hoping one of them would reply, when Brandon tapped me on the arm, "We're here." I looked up and realized we were already at my place. Fuck. The last thing I wanted to do was go inside. There was no way I was going to be able to relax until I heard from Lexi or Daphne.

Brandon must have read my thoughts and suggested we get a drink instead, and I was grateful for the distraction. I hoped he'd forgive me because if Daphne responded and was willing to see me, I was going to ditch him so fucking fast.

We ended up at a dive bar within walking distance of my place that I had been to a number of times. I liked this place. It was the perfect place to disappear to when I wanted a quick drink without being disturbed. I'd sometimes come and write here when I needed a change of scenery from my apartment. The music was never too loud, and I found the hushed whispers of the other patrons oddly soothing.

Each of us ordered our respective drinks at the bar and then retreated to a high top in a corner. "So what happened?" Brandon asked once we were settled in.

I took a breath. I didn't want to think about that asshole's hands on Daphne, so I started at the beginning. "Everything started out well. Daphne and I were catching up, and it seemed like our chemistry was still there. Then, when she went to the bathroom, that dickhead must have cornered her. I had a weird feeling that something was off, so I went to make sure she was okay, and that's when I saw his hand on her throat. I didn't think. I walked up to him, pulled him off her, and laid him out. I guess that's when you showed up. It was all kind of a blur."

"Yeah, Lexi and I were just chatting. But then she saw something that made her jump up and head toward the back. I'm assuming now that it was Daphne's ex. But I gotta tell ya, brother, posting your bail wasn't really on my bingo card for tonight, ya know? Glad I was able to get you off him." Brandon chuckled and then took a long sip of his beer. "Listen, you can't be going around knocking people out like that. This could come back to bite you in the ass, brother."

"I know, you're right, but the thought of anyone hurting Daphne just sets me off." Just then, my phone dinged with an incoming message.

LEXI

Hey, she's fine, but I think she's in shock. She hasn't been on her phone at all.

ME

I need to see her. Can I come over?

LEXI

She's pretty shaken up. Maybe just give her the night.

ME

Will you please tell her I'm here if she needs me and that I'll try her tomorrow?

LEXI

Will do. And bt dubs, good job. I've wanted to punch that piece of shit for years.

I laughed and put my phone away. "Lexi said Daphne's okay and that I should give her some space tonight. I think that's a terrible idea, but she knows her best, I guess."

"Lexi is a good friend, and she seems nice." My brother smiled and seemed to be remembering something.

I raised my eyebrow, "Nice, huh? Is that all?"

"Oh, stop. We were just passing the time. Yes, she seems

nice. That's all." Was my brother blushing? What the hell? I had to put a pin in that because my thoughts drifted back to Daphne and how scared she looked. I tipped my drink back, letting the warmth spread down my throat and throughout my body. I hoped after a few more of these, I'd be able to quiet my mind enough to get some rest tonight.

36

DAPHNE

I was in a haze as we made it back to Lexi's apartment. I don't remember the drive or walking up the steps. I was standing in the bathroom, taking off my makeup, replaying every moment from the night over again in my mind.

"I need to see him," I said, almost to myself under my breath.

"Who?" Lexi snapped. "Marcus? No fucking way."

"No, Nathan. I need to see him, Lexi. I missed him." I was staring at the mirror but not really seeing anything, thinking about how he came to my rescue at the club, a small smile pulling at the corners of my mouth.

"Babes, I think we've had enough excitement for one night. Let's get in our jammies and get some ice on that wrist." Lexi reached out and touched my hand that was holding onto my now throbbing wrist.

"I'm fine, Lexi. I promise." I finished taking off my makeup and had Lexi help me out of my corset. Once we were in our comfy clothes, she joined me on the couch with a bag of ice.

"Here, humor me and put this on your wrist."

"God, fiiiine. Anyone ever tell you that you're a bit of a bully?" I laughed and took the ice from her and placed it on my swollen joint. I was definitely going to have a bruise by morning.

After we settled on the couch, I pulled my phone out of my bag to see a single message from Nathan.

NATHAN

Hey, are you okay? Can I see you?

I sat up a little straighter and smiled. Nathan had the uncanny ability to make me smile no matter what I was going through, and that made my next decision an easy one.

ME

Hey, yourself. I'm okay and yes, I'd like to see you too.

His reply came almost immediately.

NATHAN

Are you at Lexi's? I'll come to you.

I turned to Lexi. "Nathan is coming here."

"You two are impossible. He texted me while we were in the cab too, but I told him to give you the night. Stubborn ass. Just like you." She rolled her eyes, but the smile on her face gave her away. Clearly, she was on board with Nathan and me, or she wouldn't have conspired to make that meetup happen in the first place. Lexi had a tough exterior and put up emotional walls like no one I had ever met, but deep down, I knew there was a romantic soul just dying to get out. She stood up from the couch. "If things are going to get X-rated, please go to his place. I don't need your fluids all over my couch." She faked a scowl and stomped off toward her room. Okay, maybe the whole romantic soul thing was a stretch.

Twenty minutes later, there was a knock on the door. I checked the peephole, still a little shaken up from my run-in with Marcus. I kept telling Lexi (and myself) that I was fine, but in reality, I was not okay. Marcus and I had a very tumultuous relationship, but it had never gotten physical before. I never felt truly scared of him before tonight, and I did not want to ever be alone with him again.

I opened the door and the sight of Nathan standing there cracked my heart wide open. Until that moment, I thought my heart wasn't ready. I had thought giving Nathan a shot would be a colossal mistake because I believed I was broken beyond repair. But seeing him standing there and the concerned look on his face stripped away all of my hesitations. I practically leaped into his arms.

"Oh God, Baby, are you okay?" Nathan wrapped his strong arms around me and carried me inside, kicking the door closed behind him. I nodded into his neck, but words escaped me. He placed me down on the couch and looked me over, touching almost every inch of me to check for injuries. "Please tell me you're okay."

I took his face in my hands so he would focus on my face. "I'm okay, Nathan. I'm better now that you're here."

"When I saw that asshole's hand on your throat, I wanted to kill him, and if anything serious had happened to you, I would have." He was deadly serious, and the thought of him actually killing Marcus should have scared me or been a turn-off, but it wasn't. Not even close. I was on fire for this man. I was obsessed with how feral he was in the club when he saw Marcus hurting me. Something flashed in Nathan's eyes. "Enough of this shit. You're mine," and then he met my lips. He was ravenous, devouring all of my willpower to stop him, not that I truly wanted to.

"Ahem." The sound of a throat clearing made me freeze. With our mouths still together, I shifted my eyes to see Lexi standing in her bedroom doorway with her arms crossed over her chest. "As much as I love a free show, if y'all are gonna fuck, can you please move this party somewhere else? I happen to like this couch, and I don't want to have to replace it."

Nathan pulled away from me and chuckled. "You wanna get out of here?" he asked with a boyish grin.

Self-doubt was starting to creep back in, but I decided to say "fuck it" and go with him, anyway. "Yes." I barely got the word out as I was being lifted off the couch and tossed over Nathan's shoulder. He started striding to the door when I realized I needed to grab a few things. I at least had to grab my phone and maybe a toothbrush and a change of underwear. I was laughing as I tapped him on the back. "I need to grab a few things. Give me a minute."

Reluctantly, he did as I asked and set me down. "Okay, but make it quick. We have some lost time to make up for. You made me wait entirely too long to have you in my arms again." He placed a chaste kiss on my lips and swatted my ass when I turned to walk away. "I'll be out front," he shot over his shoulder as he walked out the front door.

When Lexi and I were alone, I couldn't contain my grin. Was this actually happening? Was I really going to throw caution to the wind and jump into something with Nathan? My smile fell because now that he wasn't standing directly in front of me, I could think more clearly. All the reasons not to do this came to the front of my mind at that moment.

"What?" Lexi asked when she noticed the change in my expression.

I put my hands over my face, "What am I doing, Lexi? Marcus is clearly not over me, and I need to make sure he understands we are done before I get into a new relationship. Plus, I still don't really know Nathan. He could be just as bad. Marcus wasn't all bad in the beginning either, remember?"

Lexi pulled my hands away from my face. "You stop that shit right now. You're scared, and I get that, but Nathan isn't Marcus. Will things be all sunshine and roses with him? Who knows? Maybe things will fizzle out or he'll turn out to be a total psycho like Marcus, but you'll never know if you don't give him a shot. You can't spend the rest of your life hiding from love just because you're afraid it will fail." She let out a deep breath. "But think about it. Do you truly believe Nathan is like Marcus?"

"No. You're right. I'm talking myself out of him because I'm terrified of the feelings I already have for him, and I don't want him to break my heart. The potential is there, Lexi. He could ruin me." A fat tear slid down my cheek.

Lexi scoffed, "No man is going to ruin you. You listen to me; you're stronger than that. You will not be ruined by a man. Sure, your heart may get broken, but you will put the pieces back together, and you will keep going, and eventually, you'll find the piece that's missing. Maybe Nathan is that missing piece and maybe he's one of the pieces you'll need on your path to the right one, but your person is out there. If you don't give Nathan a shot, you'll never know whether or not it's him."

I looked at my friend with new eyes. Who was this wise woman standing before me? This couldn't be my "fuck and run" bestie, who almost never even slept with the same guy more than once. "Who are you and what did you do with Lexi?"

"Har, har, har. Laugh it up, but you know I'm right. Love may not be in the cards for me, but you fucking live for this shit, and I know in my soul that you will end up as the main character of your own happily ever after. And you deserve it, so get out of your own damn way and go get your man."

37

NATHAN

I couldn't bring myself to go all the way to the car. I knew Marcus was in jail, at least for the night, but I still couldn't bear the thought of her being out of my sight. When she rounded the corner and saw me standing by the stairs, she initially looked startled, as if she wasn't expecting to see someone standing there. But her expression almost immediately softened when she realized it was me. "Hey," she said meekly.

As she reached me, I slipped my hand in hers. "Hey, yourself." She smiled up at me, and we continued down the stairs and out to my car.

After we were inside, I turned to face her. "Are you okay for real? I know tonight was a lot, and I'm not going to pressure you to come home with me if you aren't ready."

"Nathan, I am okay, truly. Like I said, I was a little shaken up, but he didn't hurt me too bad. My wrist is sore, but it's not serious." I reached out to touch her wrist, and she quickly grabbed my hand. "Oh my God, Nathan, are *you* okay? Your hand is swollen!"

I took her hands in mine gently and gritted my teeth, "I'm fine, Kitten, except I can't get the memory of his fucking hands on you out of my head. If anything had happened to you, I don't know what I would've done."

"He didn't do any real damage. I'm okay. I just want to forget about Marcus and move on." Her eyes were glassy, but told me she was telling me the truth. Physically, she was okay. I only hoped that Marcus didn't ruin any progress we had made.

I pulled her in close and kissed her forehead. "Now, let's get you home." I meant to say "back to my place," but *home* just slipped out. I let it hang there in the air between us and didn't correct myself because the truth was, I wished it was our home.

We drove the few minutes it took to get to my place in silence with our hands intertwined. I stroked my thumb over her knuckles, thinking about the night and how things hadn't exactly gone to plan. Thankfully, the end result was the same, and I was going to do my best to keep Daphne from running off again.

After parking in the garage of my building, I led Daphne to the elevator. Once the doors were shut, I thought of grabbing her and pressing her against the wall to kiss her, but she spoke before I could make my move.

"I still don't know if I'm ready for something serious,

Nathan, but I'm willing to at least see where this goes. If you're okay with taking it slow, I'd like us to date and see what happens." She shrugged her shoulders and looked at my chest.

I don't know if she was feeling shy or insecure, or was worried about what my reaction would be. I tipped her chin up so her golden eyes met mine. "Baby, I told you before, I can wait for you to be ready."

The elevator doors opened, and I led her to my apartment. When she was in my place, she took a few moments to look around. "Wow, this is really nice." She turned from where she was standing by the floor-to-ceiling windows to smile back at me. "You've got a great view."

"Yeah, it's pretty great from where I'm standing," I laughed at my cheesiness.

Daphne laughed, "Whoa there, buddy, you want some wine with that cheese?" There she was—my quirky, funny, easygoing Daphne.

I crossed the room and hugged her tightly, placing a kiss on the top of her head while inhaling her scent. I felt so content with her in my arms, like all the obstacles standing in our way didn't exist, at least in that moment.

"Baby, I was so scared. When I saw his hands on you, I was so afraid of losing you." I let out a shaky breath. "All I wanted in that moment was for you to be okay and for us to have more time. And I know you probably still aren't ready, but I will keep showing you how much I care about you and try to make you feel safe and loved. Because you are, you know, loved." I took a deep breath and tightened my hold on her. "I love you, Daphne, and I know it's fast and probably not the best time for me to blurt it out, but I know how I feel, and I can't imagine my life without you in it. And I'm sorry if that scares you, and I'm sorry if it's too soon. But that's how I feel… No, you know what, I'm not sorry. My dad knew from the moment he met my mom that she was the one, and when I met you, Daphne, I knew there was something here. I tried to play it off. I tried to ignore it, but I knew, and I won't let you push me away. I will fight for this. I will fight for you because you're worth it and I will spend the rest of my life wooing you if you'll let me." I was still holding her tight, so I couldn't see her face.

She pushed her hands against my chest to separate us and looked up at me through thick, wet lashes. "Okay."

I stared at her in disbelief. Did she just say okay? Was this goddess of a woman going to give us a chance? "Okay?"

"Yeah, fuck it," she said as she grabbed the back of my neck and brought my face down to hers and looked right into my eyes. "What's the worst that could happen?" Then she kissed me hard, licking at the seam of my mouth until I allowed her access. Our tongues initially fought for dominance, our hands tearing desperately at each other's clothes. Then, something shifted. Our kisses became slower, more intentional, more sensual. This was the shift I'd been hoping for.

I lifted her shirt over her head and kissed down her

body, sucking one of her tight nipples gently into my mouth. Daphne let out a soft moan that had my dick straining painfully against my pants. "Damn, Baby, I've missed those sounds you make. Now I want to hear you scream my name while you come on my tongue." I squatted in front of her, taking her pants and underwear with me to the ground. As she stepped out of them, I ran my hands up her legs and looked up at her. She was beautiful, smiling down at me with so much love in her eyes. She hadn't said she loved me when I said it to her, and I didn't expect her to. She had just told me it was still too soon to get serious, but I couldn't help telling her how I felt. In that moment, I could feel that she loved me too, even if she wasn't ready to admit it out loud.

I buried my face between her legs and swiped my tongue slowly through her wet folds. "Mmm, Baby, I missed this. You taste so good." As I continued to lick and suck, she squirmed and moaned. She pulled at my hair until I released my mouth from her clit.

She tugged at my shirt. "You too, Nathan. I want to see you." I stood to my full height and dragged my shirt over my head. Daphne dropped to her knees and unbuckled my belt. With her eyes locked on mine, she unfastened my pants and pulled out my now throbbing cock. She didn't waste a second, and the next thing I knew, she was licking it slowly from base to tip, greedily tasting the bead of pre-cum that was waiting for her. I groaned. At this rate, I wasn't going to last long and there was no way I was going to come before I was balls deep inside of her.

I moved quickly, grabbing her under her arms and lifting her so her legs wrapped around me and I crashed my mouth into hers. I walked us over to the floor-to-ceiling windows and thrust into her as soon as her back met the cool glass.

"Nathan!" she gasped. "Someone is going to see!" She tried to push me away, but I held her tight with my dick pulsing inside of her, eager to be let loose.

"You can't see from the outside, Baby." I reared back and pushed into her again, harder this time, and she screamed. "That's right, Kitten, scream for me." I fucked her hard and slow against the window as she screamed my name and other expletives. I wanted to take my time with her, but there would be time for that later. At that moment, all I wanted was to feel her come all over my dick. I reached between us to rub her clit with my thumb, and within a few seconds, she came hard. I felt her tight, wet heat squeezing me with each pulse of her orgasm, sending me right over the edge with her, and I came with a roar. My cock pulsed inside of her and held her tight until I could speak again. "Sorry, I wanted to take my time with you, but I couldn't. I needed to be inside of you."

Daphne giggled, "Yeah, I got that. It's okay, I'm not complaining."

I kissed her softly on her nose and then stalked off to my bedroom with my cock still buried inside of her. "And I'm not even close to being done with you."

We spent the rest of the night making love and snuggling close together, eventually falling asleep in each other's arms. Daphne was done running away and I couldn't have been happier.

Waking up with Daphne in my arms the next morning was extraordinary. Her body was so soft and warm against mine, her gentle snores filled the air and I wanted to wake up like that every damn day.

38

DAPHNE

The next day, Nathan took me to the police station to give my formal statement and file a restraining order against Marcus. The detectives took more photos of my now fairly prominent bruising and had already gotten the video footage from the club that showed the assault. Thankfully, it was a pretty cut-and-dry case, and the detectives didn't think it would be an issue getting the charges to stick, which helped put my mind somewhat at ease. I was fairly certain that after it got out that he had been arrested and what he did, he would be facing disciplinary action from the hospital we worked at and, potentially, the medical board. I didn't want to ruin his life completely, but I couldn't just let it go either.

A few days later, Nathan sat with me when I finally worked up the courage to call my parents and tell them about Marcus and everything that had happened. I don't know why I had put it off for so long because, as it turned out, they weren't big fans of his. I was shocked when my dad said that he "never liked that guy." I didn't introduce Nathan to them yet, but it was nice having him there for moral support. Things were going so well between us, though, and I had no doubt they'd be meeting him soon.

We were practically inseparable, except for when I had to go to work, but I ended up spending most nights at his place. Lexi acted disgruntled, but I think she was secretly happy to have her place all to herself again. I still had to find a place of my own, but for some reason, it didn't feel as overwhelming anymore. Everything felt lighter somehow, and Nathan had everything to do with that.

WHEN HALLOWEEN CAME, I knew I wanted to spend it with Nathan, wrapped in his arms in front of a roaring fire, watching my favorite scary movies, and eating Chinese takeout. And that's exactly how it started.

I smiled up at him from where I was snuggled into his arms on the floor of his apartment. "I have a surprise for you."

"Oh, yeah?" he asked with a grin.

"Yeah, I'll be right back." I gave him a quick peck on the cheek and trotted off to his room, where I had a bag of my things waiting. "Stay out there. No peeking!" I called over my shoulder. I heard him chuckling as I entered his room and shut the door.

Halloween was my favorite holiday, and that meant that usually I would have dressed up for the occasion. Since we stayed in, we didn't see the point of going all out, but I had other plans. Nathan had mentioned that he liked my sexy clown costume but was sad he didn't get to have some fun with my clown alter ego, so I decided to give him his own private viewing. It took a little longer to get into it since I didn't have a hand with the corset, but when I was all put together, I stepped in front of his full-length mirror to appreciate my handiwork. Not too shabby. Nathan was going to love this.

I went to his closet to retrieve the item I had seen there a few days ago and then went out into the living room. As I approached Nathan, he was in the kitchen with his back to me, cleaning up our mess from dinner. I cleared my throat and waited a few feet away for him to turn around.

He turned, and his eyes went wide, and a mischievous grin spread across his face. "And who might you be?"

I didn't have an alter ego prepared and blurted out the first thing I could think of, "Sidney."

"Mmm, Sidney." He started toward me, and I took a step back.

"Wait!" I held up my hand and then pulled the *Scream* mask I had found in his closet out from behind my back and threw it at him with a wicked grin. "You gotta catch me first!" I yelled as I took off in the opposite direction. His apartment wasn't huge, and I knew I'd be caught quickly, but my adrenaline was still pumping. I didn't look back, but I could hear his heavy footsteps gaining on me.

I screamed about halfway down the hallway as he grabbed me around my waist. "What's your favorite scary movie, Sidney?" he growled against my ear, the mask scratching my face. I struggled to get away. I mean, not really. I wanted that man to do unspeakable things to me, but I had to at least pretend to put up a fight, right?

He spun me around and grabbed the back of my neck, bringing me in close. His thumb swept over my lips, smearing my red lipstick. "Such a pretty clown. I bet you'd look even prettier with those pretty lips wrapped around my cock." Then he leaned in closer and whispered, "If you want me to stop, just say so. Tap my leg if it's too much." And with that, he shoved me to the ground.

He looked so fucking sexy, wearing nothing but that mask and a pair of sweatpants. I wasted no time at all reaching up to free his now rock-hard cock from those cursed gray sweatpants. I looked up into the eyes of the mask as I gripped him by the base and licked up his length. When I reached the tip, I took him into my mouth and hummed. Nathan gripped my hair tight and groaned, "That's right, paint my cock red, my dirty little clown." He laughed a little at the end and I fought to keep in character too. I loved this. I loved him. Oh fuck.

I reached between my legs to relieve the ache that was building there, but Nathan grabbed my chin roughly. I looked up to see the masked man slowly shaking his head. "Tsk, tsk. No touching. That pretty pussy is all mine, but first, I'm gonna fuck that smile off your face." Then, he thrust into my mouth, and I immediately gagged at the intrusion. "That's right, Baby, I love the sound of you choking on my cock."

God, his dirty talk and the feel of his cock pressing into the back of my throat had me absolutely feral. I was so wet, and I needed so badly to relieve the pressure building inside of me. He continued to fuck my mouth as I slurped and slobbered all over him. Tears ran down my face, and I probably looked completely unhinged, but I didn't care. The sight of him standing above me, him in that mask and taking what he wanted from me, was so fucking hot that I almost came without him even touching me where I wanted him most.

"Oh fuck, Daphne," he cried out as hot ropes of cum shot down my throat. I guess he couldn't stay in character anymore. I sucked down every last drop like the good little clown I was, and then I licked him clean as he stroked his thumb under my eye. "You look so pretty like this." He quickly pulled up his pants, scooped me up and tossed me over his shoulder, slapping my ass. "But I'm not done with you yet."

Nathan tossed me onto the bed and stood over me, still wearing the mask. He cocked his head to the side and growled, "Show me what's mine, Daphne." If I didn't have makeup smeared all over my face, he might have seen me blush, but I did as he asked and spread my legs. "More."

I pulled my thong to the side as he kneeled on the bed to reach out to run a thick finger through my wet center. He hummed his approval, and I gasped as he pushed two fingers inside of me. I was so wet and ready for him, but I wanted more. He moved his thumb to stroke my sensitive bundle of nerves, and I almost levitated off the bed. "Mmm, so responsive. Tell me what you want, Baby."

"Your mouth, Nathan, please. Lose the mask." I was breathless and ready to beg if I had to. I had never wanted anyone more than I wanted him at that moment.

He ripped the mask off and tossed it to the floor. "Good girl," he murmured as he brought his face to my center and latched onto my clit with his mouth. Oh, sweet baby Cheesus. I would never tire of his mouth on me or his cock inside of me. He knew exactly what to do to get me off. He continued to lick, suck and tease me while his hands roamed my body. He flipped the top of my corset down so my breasts were more accessible and then pinched a nipple hard, sending a jolt right to my core. I was on fire and teetering on the edge of an epic orgasm when he sat up.

"Nathan, please."

"I love when you beg, Baby, but I need to be inside of you when you come." He stood and pulled off his sweatpants, allowing his cock to spring free. He climbed over me and looked into my eyes before taking my mouth with his. I could still taste myself on his lips and it made it so much hotter. While we were fighting for control with our kiss, he pushed inside of me, stretching me. "Fuck, Daphne, you feel so good."

He continued to fuck me slow and deep. Hitting a place inside of me that had me quivering and on the edge again. When he reached between us to stroke my clit, I came so hard I saw stars and my whole body was pulsating. "Oh, fuck, Nathan," I cried out as he thrust a few more times and found his release again inside of me. He collapsed onto me and held me tight. I was still wearing the whole clown get-up, including the wig. I had no idea how that even stayed on, but there we were in a heap of tulle, sweat, and smeared makeup.

A nervous laugh bubbled out of me as I tried to push him away, "I must look like a mess."

He pulled away just enough to look at my face. His expression showed nothing but admiration. "You look beautiful." I smiled while he kissed me and then gasped as he quickly scooped me up to carry me into the bathroom.

NATHAN

She was a beautiful mess. I set her down in the bathroom and stepped back to take her in. Her wig was crooked, makeup was smeared all over her face, and her corset was flipped down, her tits on full display. I couldn't help the look of adoration that settled on my face. Daphne was everything I had been looking for in a partner. She was easy to talk to, made me laugh, and was clearly full of surprises.

"What?" She eyed me quizzically.

"You are so beautiful," I replied truthfully.

"Oh, I'm sure." She rolled her eyes and turned to face the mirror. "Oh my God, Nathan, I look ridiculous!" The laugh that bubbled out of her caused my heart to actually ache. Fuck, this woman was everything to me. How did she manage to steal my whole damn heart in a matter of a few short weeks? Daphne turned and took off back into the bedroom. "I gotta show Lexi!" *What?*

I followed her as she pulled her corset back over her breasts and grabbed her phone out of her bag to take a selfie. "What are you doing?" I asked, completely clueless.

"When Lexi and I were getting ready for that party, she was talking about how she hoped someone would ruin her makeup for her and how hot it would be. I'm just taking a pic so I can show her tomorrow. I look crazy, but she was right—it's kinda hot too." She chuckled as she threw her phone back in her bag.

"I love you." The words fell from my mouth for the second time. I didn't care if she wasn't ready to hear them or couldn't reciprocate.

"This is fucking crazy." She shook her head as she walked to me.

"Is it so hard to believe that you captured my heart?" I met her halfway, taking her face in my hands.

She beamed up at me, her eyes glassy. "Actually, no. It's crazy because I love you t—" I didn't wait for her to finish her sentence. I couldn't. I picked her up, her legs wrapping around me as I took her mouth possessively with mine.

I pulled away enough to whisper against her lips, "I'm going to spend every damn day proving to you that we are the real thing, Kitten. You're it for me."

"I know."

EPILOGUE
ONE YEAR LATER

Daphne

Driving up to the cabin felt surreal. It felt like ages ago that I first met Nathan here. Nathan reached over and squeezed my thigh as if he could read my thoughts. And as I looked up into his eyes and smiled, I knew that our chance encounter over a year ago had been fate. Our paths were supposed to cross.

The last year we had spent together seemed like a dream, one I'd be so fucking pissed to wake up from. We officially started dating just before Halloween and had been pretty much inseparable since then. Things were going so well that I abandoned my apartment search and ended up moving in with him after only knowing him for a couple of months. But hey, when you know, you know, right? At least that's what his dad had said when we were introduced shortly after Nathan and I made things official.

I adored Nathan's family. We spent many Sunday nights at his dad's for dinner and enjoying time with his brothers. They welcomed me with open arms, and it was as if I had been a part of their family from the start. I only wish I had been around when Nathan's mother was still alive. From the stories they told of her, she was an amazing and beautiful person and, according to them, she would have loved me too.

When I took Nathan to meet my parents, they were a little more skeptical of our relationship, but I knew that came from a place of love and fear of me getting hurt, rather than their dislike of Nathan. They worried that things had moved too fast, and who could blame them? Things had moved fast. Of course, Nathan eventually won them over because they could see how good he was for me and to me every day. I had never been happier or more in love.

Nathan gave my leg another squeeze, bringing me back to the present as he made the turn into the cabin driveway. It was better than I remembered. The leaves on the trees surrounding the cabin had already changed colors, and the sight of them reflecting off the lake was a sight I would never tire of. I loved fall, and this was the perfect place to enjoy it.

"How's it feel to be back here?" Nathan asked as we were getting our things out of the car.

"So weird, but in a good way. I mean, it's weird to be walking in *with* you instead of walking in *on* you," I laughed.

"Yeah, let's not drop any wine this time, okay?" he chuckled as he held the front door open for me.

Memories came rushing back of our first encounter, the electricity between us, the rush I felt during our first kiss. Things were never dull or mundane with Nathan, but those first few days had been chaotic and exciting, and being here now was bringing all of those feelings to the surface again. The air inside the cabin was charged with anticipation. I turned quickly and pushed Nathan against the wall, catching him off guard.

"Do you feel it? There's just something about this place," I breathed. My hands roamed up his chest and onto his shoulders. His response told me he felt it too. He dropped the bag he was carrying and pulled me in closer, his hand on the back of my neck. Thankfully, said bag did not contain a bottle of wine this time. That was part of our first meeting I didn't feel like reenacting at the moment.

"It's not the place, Baby, it's all us." He grazed his lips over my ear and then lifted me and turned so my back was against the wall. And then his lips were on mine, and, like the first time, electricity sparked between us. Nathan was right. It wasn't this place that did that. Every time we kissed, I felt it. I felt it every time he held my hand or sent me a text while I was at work. It didn't matter where we were or what we were doing—I felt this charge between us. It was all us. Our connection was pure electricity.

He kissed me as if I were the air he needed to breathe, our tongues exploring each other's mouths. Suddenly, my back was on the kitchen island. When did he walk over there? I couldn't care less. Time and space were no longer important as he stripped my leggings down my legs. With my shoes still on and my leggings bunched up at my ankles, he threw my legs over his head and onto his shoulders, then licked my already-soaked core from crack to clit. My hips jutted up off the counter in response as a deep moan escaped my lips.

He continued feasting on me until I was writhing and squirming and panting, so close to my release. When I was on the brink, he thrust two thick fingers inside of me and curled them to hit that spot that made me see stars, and I came with a cry as my release soaked Nathan and probably the floor in front of him. I was completely spent and lay there reeling from my orgasm as he lazily licked me clean.

"Holy shit." I looked up at him as he stood to his full height and started pulling my leggings back into place. "Wait, what are you doing?" I asked, expecting that we would take things further.

"There's plenty of time for that later, Kitten. We have plans." With that, he set me down on the ground and turned to take our bags to our room. What the fuck?

Our *having plans* entailed scary movies and takeout by the fire, my favorite pastime during spooky season. I wasn't mad about it at all, but I was still so wound up. The earth-shattering orgasm on the island was enough to keep me satiated through dinner, but I was getting impatient for more.

After dinner and about halfway through one of my favorite movies, Nathan excused himself to go to the bathroom. He'd been gone for a while, and I was wondering if I should check on him. I looked to the hallway where our room was, and standing just inside the darkened hallway was a tall figure dressed in black. I let out a small, surprised screech. *Fucking scary movies.* My eyes trailed up the muscular physique and came to rest on the *Scream* mask covering the figure's face. This mother fucker.

He tilted his head to the side. "Run," he growled. And I did. Of course, I didn't make it too far, and he finished what he had started earlier on the island.

Hours and many orgasms later, we lay in bed together, laughing about how this night was just missing my sexy clown costume, when Nathan's expression turned serious.

"What?" I laughed, "Why so serious all of a sudden?"

"Do you like it here?" His question caught me off guard. Of course, I liked it here. It was where we had met, and the cabin was so cute and cozy. We had talked about it often over the past year, and the decision to come here for Halloween had been an easy one.

"Of course I do. Why do you ask?"

"I sort of bought it. Surprise!" He made a "ta-da" motion with his hands.

"Oh my God, Nathan! Seriously? When?" I couldn't believe he had bought the cabin.

"Last month. You were so excited to come here again, so I reached out to the owner. They weren't planning on selling, but after I told her our story—well, the PG version of it anyway—she said she'd be open to at least hearing my offer."

"Holy shit! It's yours? That's amazing!" The thought of

being able to visit here throughout the year had me so excited. Visions of us paddle boarding on the lake in the summer, celebrating holidays, and having cookouts surrounded by our families flashed through my mind.

"Ours," Nathan interrupted my runaway thoughts. "It's ours, Daphne. I plan on spending my life with you, and that means what's mine is yours."

A single tear slipped down my cheek while a wide smile stretched across my face. "Best. Halloween. Ever."

EPILOGUE TWO
CHRISTMAS EVE

Nathan

Daphne and I were putting the finishing touches on our tree at the cabin when there was a knock on the door. *Our tree*—I loved that we were building a life together, and that we got to have these experiences with each other. Since Halloween, we had come up here as often as we could, spending time making the cabin our own, exploring the town and enjoying the peace and quiet outside of the city. We even added additional beds in the loft to accommodate visitors better. It was our happy place, and we were so excited to share it with our families.

I opened the front door to welcome our very first guests. My dad and brothers were there on the porch, stomping the snow from their boots. "Hey guys," I greeted them. "Glad you could make it. Come on in."

My dad was the first to wrap me in a bear hug. "Wouldn't miss this for the world, son."

"Yeah, thanks for the invite. I'm excited to see the place." Dylan was next and greeted me with a fist bump.

Brandon hugged me and slapped my back. "Feels like we haven't seen much of you lately. I can't wait to see what you've done to the place."

I followed them into the living area, where they were all taking turns hugging my better half. She beamed at each of them. She had really become an integral part of our family over the last year, and they all loved her as much as she loved them.

"Can I get you guys something to drink?" I asked as I made my way into the kitchen. They each muttered an answer and joined me at the kitchen island as another knock sounded at the door.

"I'll get it," Daphne called as she went to get the door.

"Hey bitch!" I heard Lexi shout as the door opened. "Merry fucking Christmas!" The sounds of Lexi and Daphne laughing and chatting filled the whole house as they made their way into the kitchen to join us.

"Hey, Lex," I said as I gave her a big hug. Since Lexi and Daphne were so close, we all spent a lot of time together. She was part of Daphne's family, after all. "Whatcha drinking?"

"I think it's wine o'clock!" Lexi said as she made her way to where she knew the wine glasses were. She and Daphne had spent a few nights here for a girls' weekend not too long ago. "Daphs? Vino for you?"

"Sounds good," she called and went to answer the door again. "That's my parents. I'll be right back."

Her parents joined us all in the kitchen, and we all fell into easy conversation. Daphne and I already had a lasagna and garlic bread warming in the oven and the salad on the table, so we could relax and enjoy time with everyone. During dinner, the conversation was light and centered mostly around Daphne and me and our plans for the New Year. I got the feeling everyone was expecting an engagement announcement soon, and while Daphne and I had talked about it, we weren't necessarily in a hurry to tie the knot.

We had rented a cabin nearby for our parents to stay in so that they'd be more comfortable. Even with our recent modifications, the cabin was still only big enough to accommodate four or five other people comfortably. We had set Lexi up in the guest room and my brothers in the loft. So, after dinner, our parents said their goodbyes and went to get settled in their cabin for the night. The rest of us gathered in the living room for a game night.

After a few hysterical rounds of *Cards Against Humanity*, it was Dylan's turn to be the card czar, and as he pulled a black card from the pile, he chuckled, "I still can't believe you bought this place."

Lexi chimed in, "I can't wait for a summertime invite. This snow crap isn't really my thing."

"The snow's not so bad when you've got a cozy fire and good company," Brandon added, giving Lexi a wink.

What the fuck?

Lexi rolled her eyes. Dismissing him, she turned toward Daphne, "I expect summer beach parties."

Daphne laughed, "Yeah okay, I think we can make that happen, right, Babe?" She beamed up at me.

I would do anything for her. "Of course." I leaned down, kissing the side of her mouth.

"Gross, get a room," Dylan huffed.

"Great idea." I scooped Daphne up and carried her to our room. "See ya in the morning!" I called over my shoulder. I heard some chuckles and catcalls as I shut the door to our room.

MOM WOULD HAVE LOVED THIS, I thought as I sat by the fire with Daphne snuggled at my side, surrounded by the people who mattered most to us on Christmas morning. We had decided to do a Secret Santa option to cut down on the number of gifts everyone would have to buy. I made sure I got Daphne since I had a special surprise for her.

We all took turns opening gifts, and then it was Daphne's turn to open hers. I held my breath as she tore the wrapping paper. Her hand stilled as she read the paper that sat on top of the book. "Oh my God, Nathan." She looked up at me with tears in her eyes. "I can't believe you did this. How did you keep it from me?"

"I worked on it whenever you went to work," I answered her truthfully.

"What is it?" her mom asked.

"It's our story," Daphne said with a sob. "He wrote our story."

"It's only for you, Kitten. It's the only copy," I told her as she launched herself into my arms.

"I love it. And I love you." She wrapped her arms tightly around my neck and whispered, "Best. Christmas. Ever."

FIND out what happens between Lexi and Brandon in *Snowbody Has to Know,* the next book in the Seasons of Love series.

ACKNOWLEDGMENTS

To my husband–thank you for always encouraging me to follow my dreams and talking me off the ledge when imposter syndrome kicks in. You are my best friend and real life book boyfriend. I couldn't have asked for a better partner to do life with.

To Alicia–I truly don't think Daphne and Nathan's story would have seen the light of day if it wasn't for you. Thank you for being my sounding board and helping me sort out my forever chaotic thoughts. You are my best friend and I'd be lost without you. Thank you for being the Lexi to my Daphne.

To my alpha and beta readers–you hoes were the real MVPs in this process. Self doubt and imposter syndrome is a real thing and you all kept me going with your comments and encouragement. Thank you Alicia, Justine, Angela, Lucia, Valeria, Brooke, and Savannah.

To Halla and Jasmine–Thank you for answering my endless questions and keeping me organized. Best PAs a gal could ask for.

To the Smut Sluts Book Club–what started out as a little book club on Facebook for my friends, turned into my inspiration to sit down and finally write my first novel. Seeing all of the amazing indie authors doing the damn thing in there gave me the courage to try. Thanks, sluts. Love you!

ABOUT THE AUTHOR

Michele Elizabeth is a romance author, coffee addict, and certified crazy cat lady with a flair for turning everyday chaos into the kind of spicy, swoon-worthy stories you can't put down. Married to her real-life book boyfriend and surrounded by five furballs with attitude, she somehow balances writing with wrangling real life in sunny Southern California—and loves every messy second of it.

After starting her own spicy book group, she fell hard for steamy reads, and now writes her own—raw, real, character-driven stories packed with heart, heat, and just enough rough edges to keep it authentic.

By night, she works as an operating room nurse. By every other moment, she's crafting romances that'll keep you up past your bedtime.

Be sure to follow along for updates!

@michelewritesromance
on Amazon, Goodreads, FB, IG & TikTok

Check out www.MicheleElizabeth.com to sign up for her newsletter and to get first access to her new releases, bonus chapters, events, and other news.